I0627450

Sharpener from Boston

KATARINA SEDLAKOVA

WORKBOOK PRESS LLC
187 E Warm Springs Rd,
Suite B285 Las Vegas NV 89119 USA

Website: https://workbookpress.com/
Hotline: 1-888-818-4856
Email: admin@workbookpress.com

Ordering Information:

Quantity sales. Special discounts are available on quantity purchases by corporations, associations, and others. For details, contact the publisher at the address above.

Library of Congress Control Number:

ISBN-13:   978-1-963718-95-9 Paperback Version
                  978-1-965732-12-0 Digital Version

PUB. DATE: 12/24/2024

ACKNOWLEDGEMENT

My deepest appreciation to….

All those who encouraged me and helped me to finish this book.

I want to thank to my father, my daughter and Privizer family this book would not be completed without you.

ABOUT THE AUTHOR

Katarina Sedlakova graduated from the department of Slavic philology and Slovak language and literature, successfully completed her doctoral studies. She worked as a university teacher, currently works as a Slovak language and literature teacher. She is engaged in translation work and her own author's literary work for children, but also for adults, she writes poetry, prose, and dramatic texts.

SYNOPSIS

Eva lives a peaceful and relatively successful life until she remembers her old promise to a university classmate and her life is turned upside down. She will lose her home, family, friends and money. She loses everything and finds the meaning of life at the bottom of her existence through her daughter, who owes her life, to whom she owes her life.

Nobody helps a single mother when she loses her job, when she is not entitled to state support, when she gets out of the system and cannot pay her insurance premiums, when she pays rent and lives in hotels in a town where she had two houses, when her husband deprives her of the roof over her head and all her money, when he calls the cops on her and writes criminal complaints, when he makes recordings of her daughter as testimony against her, when she has to drive five hundred miles every other week for nothing, even though she can't afford a cookie for her daughter, when her father dies and her mother and her stepdaughters split everything together... no one helps her, no one else survives either...

*

They only had each other. It was hard for Eva, but she couldn't let her little daughter, who trusted her so much, down.

The only heirloom she had was an old metal pencil sharpener, which, though she had to return it twice, the third and final time she left, she took it for good, so that she would have a memento of her grandmother, with whom she was now bound by the old pencil sharpener from Boston.

Eva's whole childhood had been connected with that pencil sharpener. She had always liked to draw, and she drew a lot. Her pencil case was full of crayons, which were always first-class sharpeners. Every time she grated, she remembered the words of her art teacher, who, seeing her shading a dry bean with a dull pencil, had cursed the twisted bean, which was her worst curse word, and sent the foreman to grate the pencils.

*

It was a day like any other, though not quite... It must have been Saturday, because her husband didn't have the imagination to plan the wedding more creatively on another day. He functioned according to tried-and-true stereotypes, adapting them to his needs from time to time to smooth over some erupting problem he'd manufactured.

The bride wore a long black dress with some sort of bead-encrusted brooch. She could still get used to that, but that someone had managed to put curlers in her hair was something she tried to forget right then and there. She felt quite made up, as if she'd gone to a carnival with a mask and didn't want anyone to recognize her. But what annoyed her the absolute most were some flowers she had plastered all over her nails. Little blue tacky flowers on her baby number of nails... And the worst thing about them was that they couldn't be removed or covered up at all.

She stood in that black dress in the living room of the lady who had glued and painted it all on, even though she knew the only way she could be with her was if everyone was on a different continent, ideally in a different solar system at the very least. Normally they certainly wouldn't have met, but her man sought out people Eva couldn't even smell, and worst of all, she had to suffer them.

A lady with no taste and zero intelligence, Majchiatko, as her husband called her, was ordering them wedding rings in addition to the aforementioned decorations and wedding accessories. No one else could have probably done it, and the stores were surely all sold out, which was why Majchiatko was ordering them from the comfort of her home via the internet. This was her world of small business and shenanigans. Only now she wasn't enjoying it one bit. She was in a hurry as she did so, as if a plastic bag with a well-crafted, just-delivered parcel had been caught between the rails, and meanwhile her gaze met the driver's in the cab of the speeding train.

When the miracle came, when the hoops were delivered, Eva was surprised to find that the sender was not a hardware store or a shop with parts for a pneumatic drill. The whole device looked like a thickened nut on a scarf that was about to break all the fingers of a child's number at any moment and thread itself onto her wrist like an eternal, invisible, and weighty bond that chained her to the wall in the tower.

Endlessly she had to repeat the words of some promise she didn't understand at all, and she especially didn't want to promise something she wouldn't be able to keep tomorrow.

- I promise... - echoed through the kitchen.

- No - I promise - her husband corrected her. She could only hear him swearing in English.

- Why do I have to recite some text I don't share? What do I promise?! I say - yes - and that's it. At least the hoops are good - she looked at her small hand, now encircled by a large nut.

Was the engagement ring forgotten, or had it not made its way to the Majchiatko internet? Eva was already a bit pregnant, so they were getting married straight away. Another ring – another expense – and her husband had those properly accounted for, the receipts carefully put away, especially when it came to her and her daughter.

*

- You're done! You're on the street, - her mother said into the phone.

She thought it would be a good idea to tell her that she was expecting her granddaughter, well, and her mom just briefly told her what she thought about it and hung up the phone.

Motherhood, her mom considered, was the greatest punishment that could befall a woman. When she was pregnant, she did everything she could to get rid of that baby. She succeeded, too, but there were two of them, those children, and the other one survived. Eva survived, the first and the last.

*

They lived with Eva´s grandmother, her mother's mother. Eva had a room with dad, mom slept on the couch in the living room and grandma had a small room off the kitchen overlooking the garden she adored so much. She was already a widow when she finished the house. Grandfather had only managed to lay the foundation stone and died. The daughter from his first marriage, Ida, was studying medicine at the same time. When she came to ask for money for her school, he told her he didn't have any because he was building a house.

The grandmother then had to sell part of the garden with a small stream and rent out the smallest room to a student to pay off a loan at the bank. She worked with money, she knew how to manage and save. People in the town remembered her, she helped many of them with their applications or loan approvals.

One day, however, she was approached by an elderly gentleman who wanted to borrow a radio, the small for the kitchen, so he could listen to the news and doze off to the noontime classical music concert. The old woman then stood up, lowered her reading glasses to the tip of her nose, looked over the top of the frame, and said to him very frankly: "My dear sir, but you're getting old, what's the use of that radio!"

She had lived through the war, and the uprising[1]. She was born in a village among the mountains. From the orchard behind the house, where they later had bees, they used to walk to the meadows. The old wooden house was in the middle of the village, next to the men's tavern. The noble lords lived on the hill above the village, the serfs gathered in the tavern. In the wooden house next to the tavern they always had first-hand information so that they knew when to yoke the oxen or shake the feathers when a foreign army was approaching. Some of them ran away, others slept in the front room.

Grandma, as the oldest of five siblings, took care of everyone. It

____

1   World War II and the Slovak National Uprising (1944).

was rumored that she was not the own daughter of the other children's father, who was in America to earn money to buy the forest and fields. But only her mother knew that, who had raised five of the children herself and buried the sixth. She didn't share the work or the burden with anyone, she just did what she could to feed them. She didn't know the day or the hour, when or if their father would return. The eldest two daughters had left their native village. The other children stayed in the house to help.

Grandmother married late for the time. She was well into her thirties. She and Eva´s grandfather lived and worked in the town bank. They had one daughter, Eva's mother. Her grandmother often sighed at how often her grandfather wanted to beat Eva's mother, but she always stopped him...

They started building in the cabbage field, right next to the cemetery. Two sisters had already built their house next to their land. The older one was divorced. Her husband was locked up. He spent years in a mine somewhere in Czechia[2] for his views. When he was released, brokenhearted, he never returned to his family.

Two women escaped from a mining factory in the valley with two small children. They carried their lives, their memories, and their hopes in the backpacks on their backs. They carried quilts and woven carpets, their past and their future, a heavy, bloody past covered with chachin, woven into the colored fibers of the stepped carpets they were leaving behind, carrying a future that was supposed to be as light as the feathers in that feathered quilt. In Slovakia, they wove rugs from the remnants of their clothes to protect them from the cold of the oppressed earth when they left for America, they sewed blankets from the remnants of their men's tattered shirts so that they would have something to cover themselves with if there was no roof over their heads.

---

2   Victims of the communist regime.

The sisters were always together. They built the house themselves, just as Eva's grandmother had. But when they borrowed a glass of vinegar, they returned the glass of vinegar. The older and shorter one was bent double, never saw the sun properly, and could hardly hold the cup in her remourous hands. The younger and larger one worked in the candy store, but before she went there she took care of everyone, weeded and hoed the garden, let out and fed the chickens, and watered the little orange begonias, which gratefully walked her along the sidewalk to the street and were waiting for her when she returned at four o'clock sharp.

They were all called no other way than little and great grandmother. She was a medical student staying with them. She was from the village, and so she wouldn't have to commute to school every day, they paid for her sublet in town. After graduation, she married the great grandmother's son. She had to learn a lot, because even the landlady's son memorized some Latin names for whole life.

The youth stayed living with them in the house until they got an apartment in the housing estate. They were only children, Eva was only child too, but she raised as if she had at least ten more siblings. They grew up together. She was the only close person around, even though she was a year younger. The rest of the cast was old, or mentally old.

No one had controlled Eva in her childhood. Where she ate and when she arrived was more or less irrelevant. Mum didn't care about her. She would only notice her if someone wanted to punish her, then she would definitely join in and push her deeper into the mire she was currently in, but if they were giving her some high honors, then she would even bake a cake, even if no one would eat it, because she couldn't bake. Quick as a chameleon she could navigate and especially adapt to escalating situations, everyday life was too banal for her. She was the kind of voter who follows the majority trend but doesn't choose what is beneficial. She didn't consider herself an ordinary person, even though she had never done anything and never had to fight for anything, she floated down the hundred-foot pedestrian zone as if it had been hers for ten years.

Eva's father was in the golden era of his career at the time. If he was at home, he was always sitting at his desk writing something, and even the arrival of the Russians[3] wouldn't have disturbed him then. Well, and her grandmother, with her coxarthrosis, propped up on a stick, would never catch up with her. He always said she would outlive him. She didn't.

The checks didn't start until puberty, when she returned in the dark at fourteen from a party. From a distance, she'd already seen her mother crossing at the wicket and knew there would be trouble, even though this nurturing moment was an unfamiliar experience for her at the time. According to her mom, fourteen was the best time to begin the educational measures that grew more intense and comical with age.

- Ask her, when did she arrive? - she jabbed at her father when he appeared.

- Well, when did you come? - he asked in disgust, though he didn't care.

- At ten o'clock, - came the quiet reply, from which he could already smell the anticipation.

- I came even later, - she heard the answer that then put out the fire for the first and last time.

The neighborhood they lived in was a gardening neighborhood. Every house had a bigger or smaller garden, every neighbour wanted to show off to the other one a nice apple he had grown, grafted and left to ripen on the seventh step to the cellar. They formed a gardeners' association and Eva's grandmother was probably the treasurer because they had a gardening stamp at home. Eva liked to play with it when

---

3 Russian troops invade Czechoslovakia in 1968.

she stayed home with her grandmother. They often went on all sorts of gardening trips together as well. Eva, pensioners and discipline beyond endurance.

All she remembers from all those expeditions is some bad Hungarian chocolate they gave her somewhere and the instruction of the guide on the bus returning from the flower exhibition Flora Olomouc to get their passports ready as the Slovak border approached. The border was there before and after, but in Czechoslovakia nobody thought of going to Czechia with a passport. Everyone laughed when the guide jokingly said this into the microphone, not knowing what a great prediction he had made. It was dark and the border was not visible, but Eva thought about those words with some apprehension, as if that past with the passports could ever come back.[4]

In the garden they had cross-grafted pears, plums, apples of the latest varieties, colours and scents. Eva's father, Imrich, couldn't even walk in the garden, because if he tore off even a leaf while walking, the whole cottage would probably burn down. When he mowed, her mother followed him around like a lit torch, checking to see what he had mowed where, because her job was to plant anything anywhere so that it would be as messy as possible. She could even plant a tree between the tracks in the garage, and if Eva´s dad mowed it down, not only would she not talk to him for the whole next month, but she wouldn't even wash or give him food to eat. Actually, she didn't do that anyway. Imro used to take his dirty things halfway across the country to his cousin's house to have them washed for him, and since his wife couldn't cook at all, he didn't have to regret not giving him food to eat either.

He also had a hobby, but it wasn't gardening. He had been

---

4 Since 1993, there have been two separate states - the Czech Republic and Slovakia. During the period of Czechoslovakia, there were two separate nations - Czech and Slovak, in one state.

drinking since Eva had known him, and according to earlier born eyewitnesses, even earlier. And he lasted a lot more than the average mortal. In the village he came from, everyone drank. They had two churches, but they intermarried with each other up to the twelfth knee, usually a metre of ground behind the house.

*

Imro was small when his mother was taken to the hospital. It was wartime. She got typhoid fever. By the time her brother took her to the city in a wagon in a fever, she was already decided. She looked up one last time to see her barefoot child in the open gate.

- Ondrej, take care of Imro when I'm not here, - she begged her brother silently, her voice fading away in the noise of the rattling wagon.

- Of course I will! - he promised, although he was sure that he would bring her back in a week, two at the latest. He didn't.

His three children were waiting for him at home, but he loved his sister and he loved Imro too. Why wouldn't he take care of him?!

She knew she wasn't coming back. She didn't want to be treated. She refused the doctors' help. She was just going to die in the city, quietly, so that her child wouldn't see her, so that it would be easier for her to leave.

The war[5] and unknown illnesses did not allow them to say goodbye. All they said was that they had buried a woman in a mass grave, with the other victims of the events, and because she was young, they had placed a child at her feet. All his life Imro went to that grave, although no one knows if his mother was really there.

There was a young girl, Ulyka they called her, who served on her

---

5   World War II.

grandfather's farm. Imro was a good boy, but he missed his mother. He never got as much love as she gave him, no one played with him anymore, no one sang to him anymore. Imro's father remarried, but Ulyka was never his mother. Even sugar was hidden from him when the child wanted to take something sweet. Soon he had to leave the cottage too. He was in the orphanage for some time, until his mother's deathbed words came true, and her brother took him in to join his three children. He could hardly walk. His leg dragged behind him, but he cared for him as if he were his own. He had a small shop and sold candy to the children in paper cones. He put Imro, as the only one of his children, to study.

Eva always thought he had been wounded in the war, only later she learned that he was sitting in the yard when a bullet from a neighbour's rifle hit him while he was shooting at sparrows in a cherry tree. For the rest of his life, he dragged his foot. When they moved to town, he bought a small Trabant that he could operate with his hands. Eva would sit by him for hours as if he were her grandfather, listening to the stories of his life that he told with love and a perpetual smile on his face.

Imro had met his father by chance somewhere on his way home from school to play ping-pong, when he had come to the town to take care of the paperwork because he had bought a new house in town for his young wife and a little daughter.

- Where are you going, Imro? - he asked him.

- I'm going to school, dad - were the only words they said to each other after years and for many years at their chance meeting. At the end of his life, when he was over ninety years old, he no longer recognized his son at all. He hadn't pretended then, and after so many years of estrangement, it didn't hurt so much anymore.

*

Well, Imro drank, but he loved his youngest daughter. He took her to school. They always stopped at the milk bar in the morning, had breakfast, she got a snack, and they walked on through town together. It was hard to tell if it was up or down, because although they were going north, they were following the current of the river that ran through the basin.

Though Eva's mother had no concern for the child or for breakfast, she never arrived at work on time anyway, and always scolded the five chickens that her grandmother let out and fed in the morning.

From school Eva go to her father's work. He worked in an old building with high ceilings, creaky parquet floors and thick walls, once the seat of the famous county courthouse. The theatrically worthy hearings that took place there were then between citizen and state.[6] After long months of suspense during the pursuit, of endless uncertainty at every step, of shadows, when at every movement one was accompanied by two other shadows, with the collars of their coats turned up to their knees, and with their hats on their heads covering their faces. The same ones gathered evidence, kept records of endless phone records, and shot spotlights directly into the faces of the interrogated, crying their victims into a corner, forcing them into confessions for which they were not responsible.

- Guilty! - was the voice from behind the large and heavy door addressed to the defendant, because the state could not be guilty, nor the defendant. From the same door, first came the civil servants in their famous long coats with turned-up collars, then the well-paid, satisfied judge in the robe of "justice" and finally the citizen, so that the theater would have a paying audience.

---

6   Persecutions, fabricated accusations, interrogations, trials and imprisonment, which under the communist regime deprived people of their freedom, family, health and often even their lives.

- Guilty! - was also heard from behind the door through which Imro appeared. Guilty of treason, which he could never, but had to commit, because there was and will be no greater patriot in the republic. He rebelled and rebelled until they bent him, but never broke him.

In the same hallway, but a quarter of a century later, hung a wonderful mirror where Eva's first choreographies were created, but the main thing was in her father's office. He always had sugar cubes in his cabinet. They were the best and sweetest that a child with his endless imagination can imagine. And sometimes they were even colorful. She would wait for him at the typewriter, on which she had written her first poems. It wasn't so much about the poems as about writing, because she enjoyed it. It reminded her of playing the piano, and when her fingers hit the letters of the typewriter, she would look for rhythm in it. She would tap her fingers as if they were on piano keys and arrange the song on the paper in poetic images.

They didn't have a piano at home and they certainly wouldn't buy one for her, so she played on the typewriter. Once, her father's colleague from the next office commented on her concert, saying that it reminded him of a woodpecker pecking at a tree. She wondered how the large tapestry on the wall could have disappointed her so much and let out a few notes to it, so she relaxed her poetic passion for a moment, but only for a moment. Her father had to read her poems after every change the author made. He didn't want to, but he had to. Sometimes she would recite them to him on the way home. However, the golden era of her poetic work came a little later, when she began to write her own poems in Russian. More precisely - about one. Then her nationally oriented father "tidied" her up to his place, to his Slovak "shelf".

They didn't go home so directly as to school. Accompanied by her father's favorite colleagues, usually the same ones, with the same hobby as Imro, they went on a tour with several stops in the three-meter pedestrian zone. These were cafes where smoking was still allowed at that time and where children never went, but no one bothered when she was there. After all, if someone tried to say something to Imro, the comb in the form of a hairpin over his bald head would quickly bristle into the desired shape on the cockerel and the friendship would be over.

The buffets had high tables, which people stood at, probably so that people wouldn't stand there for long, because the republic needed sober citizens. Those tables had a shelf where they put bags, gloves, umbrellas, and hats. Everyone stood there in their coats, because it wasn't warm there and there wasn't much space to put them. These establishments didn't have the French nobility back then, but the family atmosphere was felt at every step, especially when friends said goodbye and hoped to see each other again soon.

Father with his friends and glasses of wine leaned steadily on top, Eva with a mayonnaise salad on the bottom shelf, where spilled liquid from the upper floor dripped onto her on the rubber tablecloth. She grew up with the smell of spilled wine and salty potato chips in her nose, and she honestly hated it all her life. Father forgot everything on the bottom shelf. Lots of umbrellas, hats, and gloves. But Eva was valiantly pursuing him, and not just for the moment of poetry that she almost always had ready. It was the instinct of self-preservation that drove her, because she knew what it meant to be forgotten.

Her father finally managed to buy an umbrella with a handle that resembled a duck's beak. He never forgot that umbrella anywhere. More precisely, that umbrella always came to him, just like Eva, and after Imro's death, it, along with his literary legacy, ended up in a museum to live on and tell his great story.

*

It was Christmas. Eva's daughter's first Christmas without a roof over her head. After six moves in two months, she was strapping her baby back into her car seat and loading the few belongings they had. The Boston´s sharpener was already traveling with them.

They were moving south. The roads, buried in snow, were strewn with sea sand. Tiny shells, glistening in the spotlight, could be collected as souvenirs. They passed one of the dams that had been built in the last century. They were drowning villages, streets, houses, and memories. The water level was noticeably low, lower than usual. A church tower from it on the horizon. She stopped and rolled down the window. The child was asleep. She looked at the tower of the extinct church and thought she could hear the bells. As if the wind had wandered into the tower and set time in motion.

It was a silent winter, the village was covered in snow, with no signal and no contact. People no longer met, only the closest neighbors shouted something to each other when they shoveled new snow in the morning. No one went to the shop, or even to the pub in the center of the village. Every house had at least one cow, they baked bread and warmed themselves with homemade brandy. If they had a pig, the sow was always called Duda, if it was a boar, it was called Gruchy. The piglet was served regularly once a year in the so-called Christmas cycles, with the name bacon, schnitzel or sausage. Almost every second donkey in the village was called Vichor.

A small old van arrived at Vinco´s threshing floor, which stood at the intersection of the last two streets below the mountain, early in the morning. The driver lowered the side wall and the car, which was already waiting for a frozen crowd of people, turned into a mobile shop, where you could buy everything, from flour to underwear, even with a try-on. In addition to goods, it also transported more daring travelers from one hill of the village to another. The driver and salesman in one person never used a cash register or a calculator. By the time a person had made up his mind about what he wanted to buy, the resulting amount was already on his tongue.

A clever businessman, adapted to local conditions, did not let a nation, accustomed to similar and greater calamities for years, perish. If nature did not frighten them, the state held a raised finger and at regular intervals announced some kind of emergency. People often had their water turned off with an announcement that it was unknown when it would be turned on, or that it would be turned off for at least twenty four hours. For this reason, every house had a year-round supply of water and bottles of preserves. Who would build a flush toilet when the latrine could be used even if the water wasn't running? And in the end, it's not even clear whether it was real or just another rehearsal.

She always liked that down there, in the south, the weather was a month ahead, nature woke up to summer earlier and even the rainy days didn't last as long. But then she also thought about the possible disadvantages that could result from that, whether they simply missed that month. There could be various complications associated with that. On the other hand, it also brought a lot of advantages and improvisational possibilities. It's not that easy to do all our normal human duties, such as birth, growth, adolescence, aging and death, in a shortened mode. It could happen that some phase is skipped, forgotten or neglected in that speed. But it's certainly nice to get twelve salaries in eleven months.

*

Aunt Kata used to come to Vinco's house on Sundays. She lived with her parents in a house full of cats. She had a rented cafeteria in the center of the village, where she made coffee and held small parties, which in the local context were large-scale events. And if it weren't for these cultural events, she would have gone completely crazy herding goats, herding sheep, and raking hay.

After one such party, there were balloons left in the cafeteria at the aunt's. She called Vinco's house so that the child could choose from them. The offer was truly rich. The child subjected almost all the specimens to a stressful test and took the winning, most durable one with her. She proudly walked up the street with it. In her small hands, she squeezed a large colorful bubble, from behind which were sticking out her naughty boots and three pink pompoms, probably from a hat that could not be seen. After a few meters, when the climb became more difficult, and the attention of the little girl with the big balloon was more focused on the ascent than on the precious treasure, the balloon was freed from her hands and after a short maneuver in the air, the balloon went to look behind the school fence. The misfortune and the child were left standing on the road. They looked as if someone had just taken the world from them. In addition to the pompoms on the cap, one could also see immense disappointment, a tear-stained gaze, fixed on the receding object, and a heartbreaking cry was about to break out on the wrinkled child's face. The child stood there and patiently waited for her balloon. Not another, only her own.

At the same moment, a farmer appeared on the road. An old man, with the last tooth of a kind smile, burdened with six bags and a stick in his hand. His goats were grazing somewhere in the meadow, and in the meantime he had run off to the village. He saw the child from a distance and felt in the air the great misfortune that had befallen him. He left the goats as goats, the village as village, and decided to help his new little friend. With all those bags on his shoulders, neck, and belly, he started jumping and chasing himself with a big heavy stick. The child quickly got his bearings in the improvised situation and appreciated the friend's efforts with an enthusiastic scream and a joint jump. For a moment, it seemed as if the balloon had also come to take a look out of curiosity. It flew around the old man, soaring and sinking, the child screamed and people stopped to rest, because they could no longer walk with laughter. When it seemed that fate was on their side, when the balloon also began to fly almost to the ground, the air bubble in the colorful wrapper suddenly burst. It caught on an invisible tip and flew into a thousand small red pieces, which then lay soulless on the ground.

*

The cat house, where Vinco's wife Tatiana also came from, was visited on the second Christmas holiday. It got warmer and it started to rain. The car was always used to go to the second hill in the village. This time, it was a two-person trip. They were having dinner. The child was sitting on the bed among her toys. Treats called pork bacon, schnitzel or sausage were not yet her thing. The program was just about to include some free entertainment when a woman, a character named Aunt Kata, came on stage to inform those present that the rain had turned into snow, and quickly left again so that her lit cigarette, her closest friend, would not burn out completely.

Simona, the daughter of Vinco and Tatiana, was driving home. The narrow bridge was sunken and even narrower than usual. The car skidded into the ruts and drove through a narrow passage over the empty bed of a lost stream. She scrambled uphill, but didn't brake down. Tires bitten into the snow bounced along the unploughed road. Freshly fallen snow buried the neighbor's deaf dog, which was sleeping by the road. The wheel of Simone's car caught the sleeping animal. Another pair joined the helplessly pleading dog eyes in the dust of the road.

*

Vinco and Tatiana worked in three village clinics, where they sometimes treated or just pulled out some teeth or removed their remains. Usually, they were visited by cleft-faced old women, who widened their gaping smiles, pulled out superfluous teeth and their roots, or pulled out nerves weakened by years, time, and stress. The clientele who visited them was no longer interested in overpriced white fillings, braces, or porcelain crowns. This generation needed to get rid of their teeth and other partially immovable assets, and especially the problems with them.

Let others worry now, I'll rub my dry crust into milk and nothing hurts. I've also been sleeping better since I didn't have them, - they talked to each other in the waiting room.

The dentist in forgotten, almost extinct villages was more of a notary than a dentist. He was putting in order ordinary human things that a person does not take to the other world. No one needs a bright smile there.

*

It was late afternoon when a figure in black rang the doorbell. Instead of a bell, a dog barked to announce the visitor. Aris, a large shepherd dog, hated visitors. He knew exactly who he could let in and who should not even look at the doorknob. He had been limping since he was a child. Someone had kicked him, someone he knew and trusted. No one could come near him anymore. He had been kicked with his right hand, from behind, and from then on he made a distinction between family and acquaintances.

Even that day, no one would have rung the doorbell if he hadn't had a tight chain for short distances. The black figure behind the gate belonged to a young monk from a nearby monastery. He urgently needed a dentist. Everyone knew Vinco and everyone knew that he could come to him at any time if Aris would at least let him in at the gate. On Fridays and holidays, the drill would growl and growl, usually for a good word for acquaintances and the poor from all over the area. Tatiana did the administration, and she would go to urgent cases only when Vinco could not be found anywhere. Only Tatiana knew how to write down the reconstruction of her grandmother's teeth on the health cards collected from the nearest neighbors. Only she knew how to write out the tables for the bottomless health insurance company in a way that would make her see the bottom. In exceptional cases, Simona, otherwise very lazy, usually sleeping daughter, helped her with this when it came to work. It was better if she did nothing, at least there was nothing to fix.

Vinco was just with the cows when Aris started bleating. He didn't hear himself say a word, but he promised to come. He and

Tatiana milked their six cows three times a day so that they wouldn't waste milk. They always came to them in clean, ironed clothes, perfectly matched, with a scarf or shawl around their necks to honor those mute, grateful cattle. Vinco milked the last cow. He didn't change, he just wiped his hands and went to see his worthy father. Instead of his father, however, his son was waiting for him in the armchair. Anyone who didn't know them would say they were brothers. The difference between them was no more than seventeen years. Both were young and fresh, with smiling rosy cheeks.

*

The child was asleep when she for first time arrived at the monastery. There was only a monk and two helpers who were helping with repairs. Milos, a friend of Vinco's family, decided to show her around. The monastery was nearby. They jumped off. The area consisted of several old, self-helped buildings that were forever being renovated, an outbuilding, and clucking hens warming their claws on the top stone of the church steps. The monastery was in a desolate state when the young man, full of ideals and reforms, arrived there. The water was turned off, the electricity was unpaid, and the walls, rotted by years of dripping water, were now creatively decorated with mold. She crept along the worn-out paths in the leaky roof and gradually made a home out of her temporary residence. Her temple silence, peace, and comfort were only disturbed by a fresh wind that opened the windows and drew the scent of melting snow into the musty spaces. Radical repairs began. The chapel, the ground floor of the residential area, and some rooms upstairs were gradually renovated. The hens began to run around more cheerfully, and visitors who came in with a shovel also received coffee in their second hand.

A hungry person dreams of food, a thirsty person dreams of wine, and Eva longed so much for a roof over her head that she subconsciously asked Milos if she could stay in the monastery. He didn't know, but when the monk sat them down on a bench on the wall, he asked. The question from two young people who just happened to go to God's tent was answered:

– I don't rent rooms for a few hours.

*

Then it was time for Simona's teeth, which required professional cosmetic surgery. She decided to replace her six front, yellow and crooked ones with shiny white porcelain crowns. The only problem was that it had to be done right away so that she wouldn't have to deal with it for a long time and walk around the world with the smile of an old beluga. It didn't work. The teeth were filed right away, but instead of a shiny smile, she had to walk around for some time with filed teeth, between which you could easily fit five white, thin cigarettes at once, while they made custom-made porcelain jaw accessories for her. In addition, she had a new hairstyle and started decorating her face in the morning. And all this just because she could find a man, because the further you get past thirty, the harder it is.

Eva has always considered the unpleasant thick black hairs on the chin, which young women have removed and which irritate us in old women, to be an unwritten sign of aging, because they no longer remove anything, more precisely due to poor eyesight and obesity, they only remove what they see and what they can reach.

There were several candidates for marriage, but none of them was the right one, the ideal one, the one she dreamed of. Instead of a groom, hormones spoke to her students, who began inviting her to various events with the hope that these measures were taken because of them. And so it happened that she had two invitations to one opening. She rejected the student's invitation in the morning so that she could come to the same event in the evening with an invitation from work. Her student also came there. He was accompanied by a small, broken-at-the-end elderly lady with a cane, who had arrived because of his invitation.

The potential groom in this story was Milos, although there wasn't actually any wedding. Milos was a lawyer in his brother's firm, which had numerous branches in southern Europe. However, he was not the perfumed handsome man in a pressed suit, with gelled hair and polished shoes, for whom crowds of long-legged girls in expensive fur coats and leather boots await, with a fifteen-centimeter skirt around the waist in summer and a seventeen-centimeter skirt around the waist in winter.

Milos only had a company car, which was quite visible. He had a suit hanging there when he went to work, a bag with toiletries and a spare set of clothes. The only drawback was that there was no running water, so he lived in his parents' apartment. The family had received it from the head of the demolition team for a demolished house in the same neighborhood. It used to be a suburb of the capital with family houses, now a dark, dirty neighborhood with scribbled apartment buildings and unlit subways. When they were demolishing their parents' house, his grandfather stood there and watched the devastation until the end. When they finished, he too breathed his last. The place where their old house stood was on the corner of a newly built street, where they later lived. Several times a day, year after year, they walked past the site of their family tomb. Out of piety, Milos lived his entire life in a museum. He didn't change anything about his exterior or interior. He slept in his parents' beds, used their closets, and the things he wore smelled of a mixture of mothballs, geraniums, incense, and vinegar, which he sometimes used to clean his iron.

He regularly spent all weekends, except four a year, with his mother. On Saturdays, he would shop for her, on Sundays he would go to church, where he would gradually take all his things and then watch TV with her all afternoon. He had lost almost all his friends, but he was probably happy. Only Vinco's family and Simona were left to him. He could come there at any time, and those were his four remaining weekends without his mother. He had known Aris since he was a puppy. He was the only one who hadn't been bitten by that big, wronged, good guy.

Milos was an acquaintance of Simona's sister. They met one morning, on their way to work. They lived together for a short month. Everything went faster somehow, as if they wanted to catch up on something that they wouldn't have time for later. It was raining and his car had broken down. He was standing at a bus stop. His dusty shoes were wet and now muddy, along with his socks. He didn't have an umbrella, because he never carried one. This day wasn't the right one to make an exception either. He didn't hide under the roof, because there wasn't one nearby. He could only rely on a small, fast minibus that might appear at any moment, so that he could start waving at it at the right moment. With a bit of luck, it was possible to assume that the driver would notice him and stop.

There was water everywhere by the time the minibus arrived. It could easily have been poured out of his shoes. These were obviously waterproof, they didn't let water back in, and the higher they were, the deeper he stood in the water, from which there was no escape. He would have to completely redo the documents in his bag, which he was already late with. Completely wet, with the water he was carrying in his shoes, he sat down in the first available seat. There was only one in that small, movable space. It was a seat by the path, right behind the driver. Almost immediately he felt the water evaporating from his clothes, starting to mix with his own sweat and some perfume he had rubbed off on yesterday. It was a good thing he had gone into town by car in the evening, otherwise the mixture of smells would have been compounded by the alcohol fumes. He began to wriggle in the pool of his own water that soon formed beneath him. The minibus rattled him roughly, and he was thrown from one side to the other. When the train turned right, the wet, crumpled, smelly and disheveled Milos fell to the left, straight into the lap of his neighbor. The water from under his ass spilled out, he was obviously relieved, and that was when he saw the most beautiful smile in the world. At the same moment, he also promptly tried to show a similar expression of happiness, and his face instantly lit up with the broad smile of the last living waterman, who must have his feet in a basin of cold water, but he doesn't mind at all.

The girl by the window was smiling. She was smiling at the whole world, and it seemed to Milos that the smile belonged only to him. By the time he got out, he had a piece of paper with her phone number in his pocket, which, of course, had gotten soggy and was no longer usable. It was her last day at work before vacation.

The next day she was traveling to the seaside. Somewhere in a resort in the south, her boyfriend was already waiting for her. She was leaving with the hope that the rain would pass and the sun would shine for days. On the way, she stopped by Simona. They had a quick coffee together. Simona only said that she had to introduce her to someone.

Everything else happened very quickly, as it usually does in the short months of a short year. The sea, the sun, the chills, unconsciousness, the transfer and… nothing. Nothing more. Nothing more.

Milos waited a week, then another, and when he finally decided to call, it was too late. Someone on the phone told him that the girl with the most beautiful smile in the rain was no longer there, and that she would never be. Somehow she had prematurely done what was needed, matured, and left forever.

He got in the car and went looking for her parents. He found a village. He found Vinco's house. They had barely smiled when they were already crying again. He told them the story of the girl in the minibus. It inflamed their wounds. It made them cry. They accepted him. He came to them as if it were home. He had no one and in Vinco's house he found kindred spirits.

For Simona, he was an acquaintance of her sister. They had been on a few pleasant vacations, going skiing together, or to the seaside. One day, while they were wandering around like this, Milos took out a small box with a ring and asked Simona to marry him. She was young, she wasn't ready for something like that, and Milos wasn't the one she wanted to stay with forever. At least not at that moment.

They remained friends, connected by the seemingly invisible bond of Simona's sister and casual sex. Once, when Simona was lying contentedly in Milos's bed, straightening the pillow under her head and waiting for Milos to return from the bathroom, she suddenly jumped up. In a split second, she went from a horizontal position to a vertical one. She stood naked in the middle of the room, looking at the pillow and shouting at Milos, who couldn't hear anything through the closed door, the splashing water and the hood of his own world. She pulled the sheet off the armchair, twisted around in it and returned to the bed. She picked up the pillow and shouted at Milos even more forcefully. When he came out of the bathroom, she was already holding a glass bottle in her hand and rushing towards him.

- What is it? - she shouted.

– It's the soil from your sister's grave – came the answer after a while, which he still hears to this day.

Simona took a deep breath. She stopped screaming. She got dressed and went outside. She needed to walk and think so she wouldn't kill him. She went down the stairs, walked around the apartment building, passed Milos's family tomb, and headed to the market, which was just starting to decompose on the next street. It was Sunday and they didn't sell anything except flowers. The last time she had seen so many flowers, types, and colors was probably at a graduation party. She had originally headed there with the plan to buy carrots. Every morning she tried to drink at least a glass of fresh carrot juice. Gradually, this occasional ritual turned into a habit, stronger than drinking coffee in the morning.

She walked a lot until she found a vegetable stand in that jungle of flora. To tell the truth, she found two stands, but only one had carrots. The saleswoman was unloading boxes. She told her to come in fifteen minutes because she hadn't unloaded the carrots yet. If there had been three stalls and at least two of them had carrots, she would never have returned. But that day she had to. So she gave the woman another twenty minutes to unload the boxes and especially her carrots. She spent twenty minutes of her life walking around the vast flower exhibition. When she saw her carrot seller smoking a cigarette at the stall from a distance with a coffee in her hand, she headed over to her and without any introduction asked for half a kilo of carrots. The woman turned slowly towards her, took a drag on her cigarette and hissed at Simone from behind a curtain of smoke that she should have come in half an hour, that she hadn't had time to unload everything yet. That was really enough for her. Without a word, she turned around with the speed of someone who had been electrocuted, headed to the nearest vegetable market and bought apples.

After a long walk through the relatively fresh air of the big city, exhibitions and shopping, Simona returned to Milos's apartment. She made herself some apple juice, gathered her things from around the apartment, and went to the station to wait for a bus. Milos didn't hold her back. He didn't even dare to speak. He waited for instructions. He knew these storms and knew that this was no time to add fuel to the fire before it burned out.

Simona was silent. She stopped arguing with Miloš, stopped responding. Milos, as an object of interest for her that day, ended. He often called her, came because the door to her parents' house was always open, but nothing else. Simona registered on a dating site and started looking elsewhere.

After the holidays, Milos said goodbye. Lent began and he disappeared from his everyday sinful life. He fasted. He starved. He prayed bent over in front of the refrigerator, giving thanks for every bite he could eat. He called, but he no longer went to Vinco's house.

Honestly, he began to miss that absent-minded little man with a big heart.

On Easter, when they went to burn candles at the cemetery, there were flowers on her sister's grave and fresh footprints in the wet dirt. Random people saw a figure in black leaving, and word spread from the monastery that they had someone new there.

*

It was getting warmer. A mighty river of melted snow was rushing down the valley. Vinco started the mill and Simona drove Eva and her daughter up to see the twisted old stones. The ground corn was supposed to be made into a cake that evening. Simona didn't wait. She couldn't. Her nervous system was still on alert, always ready for stimuli to unexpected reactions that a healthy person wouldn't even notice. Before the corn was ground, Simona remembered the pots with lunch on the stove, the dog locked with the roast turkey in the same room, and she hurried to who knows where…

Eva, with a bag of flour on her back, in flip-flops, and with the child in her arms, slid down the rutted and muddy forest path with tongues of snow sticking out maliciously. She thought in her mind about the right place to calm restless human souls. When we start disappearing one by one, I guess it will become clear that we don't need to be looked for, like those lost swarms of bees that just needed to rest.

*

A woman walks into the gray building of the district court. She has been going there for twenty years, she knows the way by heart.

- Hello, Klarika! - she greets the woman behind the window familiarly, so that she will not be forgotten since yesterday and will not remain unnoticed by the eyes of the two doormen who always hang around at the entrance to the best-guarded district court in the world. Normally, she would not even notice them, but because she needs their discretion, she smiles at them with a Hollywood smile "on two fingers", generously gifted with hopelessly crooked teeth, which not even the best jaw orthopedist could put in their place.

Her massive body, shaped like the forms of a top party girl, is almost running up the stairs to the second floor, carried by two thick legs, similar to the trunks of old trees, in well-worn shoes, which in the past would have supported the ceilings of the generous tombs of sadly famous monarchs. Only the symphony of footsteps echoes across the empty, gray pavement of the corridor, as if one of the pillars were made of metal and the other of stone. The sound stops in front of the door marked Post Office and the figure enters without knocking. Despite her clumsiness, she closes it behind her quite skillfully. She looks to make sure it is closed properly and with another glance she runs around the room to see if only those she needs are there.

- Etelka, - she takes a deep breath, all red and stuffy, in colder weather, wisps of smoke would surely be coming out of her nostrils, which are now rapidly contracting and expanding.

- Do you remember that argument about the little house your parents had with your brother...? - she starts slowly and without greeting. In the pauses, she squints her eyes and spreads her hands affectedly. At the end of the sentence, she makes a dramatic pause to savor her superiority.

Statistician Etelka has been filing, numbering and distributing delivered documents at the district court for forty years and would like to have at least ten more years to save up for her retirement and be able to enjoy the house she bought with Katka's help. Another time, her fiery red hair lost its glow after an unannounced visitor arrived. Rather reluctantly, she put the ceramic file, mirror and tweezers in a drawer, but only for a while, until her visitor closed the door on the other side again.

- Of course I remember! It cost me a lot ... - Etelka remembered this every time the lawyer's footsteps, the heels of which were missing, could be recognized among the thousands, sounded in the gloom of the gray corridor of the district court.

But Etelka was not in good shape today either. While she was in court, her front tooth broke, but because all the money went to the lawyer, and some to the judge, there was no room for cosmetic maintenance, and it always looks better in court when you come there as a poor man even with a broken tooth. Well, she held on, and when it was all over and the house was transferred to her name in the land registry, she saved up money to have a crown made for her front tooth.

She had been to the dentist in the morning. He had the tooth ground down, made an impression, and scheduled it for Thursday.

- Of course I remember! – she repeated now with a wide, radiant smile.

- Well, from now on you will keep track of every shipment with this file number – and handed her a piece of paper. Etelka placed it in the central place of her desk under the glass so that she could see it from all sides.

– If anything comes up, you will let me know immediately without registering it anywhere – the instructions were clear.

*

They had that "memorable" day in an old church building. Each of the guests brought food with them. Her husband, whom she had known since college, always told her that they would get married when she was thirty-five. She didn't believe it. He was already divorced when they met, but they stayed in touch after school, even though their paths diverged.

Eva always said that when Imro gave his youngest daughter in marriage, all of Slovakia would have fun. It wasn't fun. Imro couldn't entertain his beloved nation the way he wanted and share his joy with them. He wasn't happy. His daughter wasn't getting married at home.

She was getting married in an old house near the church, in a black dress. She looked at the procession of wedding guests who, according to instructions, brought food to her wedding and she felt like crying. She didn't need half of those people at all and she could do without the other half. At least she arrived late and could make excuses for the seller of her wedding bouquet of red roses and the bride's veil, who had not made it on time.

During the wedding, she had the feeling for the first and last time that her husband had noticed her as a person. It was the moment of his promise, followed by a momentary interest and then only ridicule. She never saw that look again, after all, how many times does a normal person have a wedding and with the same person?! Before and after she was just air, used up for nothing short of a month in the year.

After the wedding, her husband's speech followed. Then Eva was supposed to turn around for the second time and leave forever. She didn't leave. In words that he probably recycled from his speech at his first wedding, he denied several times that he had ever said anything about them getting married one day, saying he was drunk at the time. He was white, she was black. He stood in a white shirt, she, Eva, first and last, in a black dress.

*

After finishing school, Eva went to the university. She lectured and, on the side, earned a small doctorate, defended her dissertation, and went to work at a university abroad. There, her husband, whom she was to marry that day, found her. She was already a little pregnant, as she said, a little over five months. Today she knows that it was a mistake. She should have listened to him when he told her that he would pay for the abortion, that she should get her period in Canada, who knows whose child it is… and similar nonsense, to get rid of responsibility. He succeeded. He got rid of the responsibility, the family, the child, and the obligations, but he kept the advantage - to dispose of the child's property. The child miraculously survived, but Eva raised him alone. Instead of enjoying her daughter's successes, she had to fight for survival and sue her father, who had meanwhile gone to Canada, lived in some barn, and paved Canadian sidewalks, if he couldn't manage that.

*

After the wedding, Eva woke up as if in another world, a world without colors and without scents. She was not closed, but she was not free either. There was emptiness around her, no friends, no one close to her, she did not consider her husband's friends as people who could ever help her in anything. They were not friends, they were just acquaintances who would disappear from life as quickly as they entered it. Eva was not attracted by the lucrative job prospect of paving bathrooms, toilets and sidewalks in Canada, and she did not want to live as a refugee without any support. She boarded the first plane and flew away.

A few weeks before the birth, she bought an apartment so that she would have somewhere to bring her child from the maternity hospital, but her husband did not like the fact that he would no longer have access to her money, so he forced her to sell the apartment and transfer the money, which she never saw again, to his account. In court, he claimed that he did not remember it. Like a movie, all his lies and distorted truths that he had told for nine years during his studies, which normally last five years, played out to her like a movie.

Eva had a daughter. Her husband's relatives, whom she had seen for the first time, came to visit her in the maternity hospital. In the maternity hospital, where something new and good is usually born, Eva's parents met her husband's mother and brother for the first and last time. By a strange coincidence that she was very happy about, Eva's father was never called father-in-law by her husband. For a person who does not notice change, his first wife's father was still his father-in-law.

Eva even once attended a visit to his first wife's grandmother. Stupidity and an attempt to show her greatness, and also technical reasons, because she could not leave even if she wanted to. From the story, she heard about an old woman who she felt sorry for. However, she was only a little older than Eva's mother and Eva was not interested in her at all. Why should she? After this mistake, however, she did not allow herself to be manipulated any longer. When her husband visited her in the hospital again, her relatives took her to the other side of the country.

*

After her father, her daughter was the only close person Eva had in the world. She was the meaning and strength that helped her move on. She laughed when it was so hard and with the lightness of the lost feathers of city pigeons that she collected for her, she helped her carry all the burden she was carrying.

A period of endless moving began. In other words, Eva lived and her daughter grew up in a car. She breastfed and changed her diapers at a highway rest stop. Her parents each lived in one house. Eva's mother managed to get her husband and her only daughter to move to a cottage. However, when her father fell ill at the end of his life and was dependent on his wife's help, there was no longer room for Eva. Her mother would not let her into the empty house, although Eva asked, the answer was unequivocal - No!

They went to Simone and her parents in Bulgaria for Christmas. To a godforsaken countryside, where they forgot all their worries, problems and unpaid bills. What was a mother on maternity leave, without an adequate man and parents, supposed to pay for them?!

When her daughter was two years old, her father came to visit them. Eva rented an apartment, diametrically different from the one she was supposed to live in with him in Canada. This one was large, bright and spacious. She had it painted, bought new carpets everywhere and foam under them. Her husband did nothing and nowhere. Eva paid the rent, they went on vacation twice a year, which he also did not remember, because Eva's expenses were not among his carefully stored notebooks.

Her daughter was not even three years old when Eva set up a kindergarten for her, right next to the job she had started. It was a few days after she learned that her husband was setting up a kindergarten about fifteen kilometers from the city and that she could drive her there every day and walk to pick her up.

She would get up at five in the morning. She washed and dressed in the dark so that her rent wouldn't increase, which her husband, who was sleeping in the kitchen on the table or on the floor by the lighted lamp, would raise quite a bit. Then she woke up and dressed her daughter. They walked together across the city center to the kindergarten and talked about the pillows in the sky. She was the first to go there, and until the kindergarten opened, she would wait at Eva's work and play on the big black wing until no one was there.

Eva worked at the national treasure depository, a building guarded on all sides, where she felt safe. She shared an office with a colleague who had previously worked in the state security services. For his faithful service, his ability to monitor everything and report everything to the right places, he earned a new four-room apartment at that time. He had two types of clothes, a winter version and a summer one. Nothing changed throughout the year in the two collections, which consisted of a knee-length cloak or coat with a raised collar from its "golden era", trousers and a beret in a thicker or thinner version.

Every time he arrived at the office in the morning, Eva was already there and had time to take her daughter to kindergarten. He got up at eight o'clock sharp. He turned on the Green wave on the radio to keep an eye on the current traffic situation, started shuffling his feet on the creaking wooden floors to take off his shoes, turned on his computer, which whistled to the entire building that he was doing something wrong, and when he couldn't fix it, he went to make coffee and made phone calls until the end of working hours, or went to accompany a conversation if he was called.

Eva promised herself that she would never do this. She didn't. However, after an undemanding and well-done job, Milanko could return to his four-room apartment with satisfaction. Eva picked up her daughter from kindergarten and they slowly walked back along the pedestrian zone, waved to the saleswomen in the sports shop, went to look at the fish in the small bakery with jam buns and very reluctantly approached their rented apartment.

Eva's husband was on a long vacation. When they returned, he was lying in the bathtub or listening to some nonsense on the computer to pass the time. She didn't eat lunch, but she brought him meal tickets from work. She found them all lying in the kitchen when she moved. They were unused and unusable. Once in a while, when she wanted to go to the theater, she had to wait for her husband to return from his afternoon run. And when she worked on the weekend, he went swimming in the pond. All she wanted from him in life was to tile her bathroom in the apartment she had owned for a while, but it was better to sell that too.

Only her father was a bright spot in this story. He had poor eyesight, but they went to lunch together every day. He spoke so normally, matter-of-factly, and understood what she was saying to him for the first time, even though it seemed like he was from another time. He couldn't see, he tripped over everything, but he was glad to be among people. He helped her with the rent, because he knew her salary wouldn't be enough, and he never mentioned her husband.

*

In the midst of all the turbulence, her great childhood friend Tibor appeared at that time. Once he came with his mother's urn, which he left waiting in the hallway, another time he called to come and get his car because the police had stopped him. In the past, people would walk around with the remains of saints when believers wanted to save them, because they believed in their miraculous power, and in Tibor's family there was a tradition of keeping the deceased in urns on a shelf in the apartment, although their miraculous power was not confirmed.

His grandfather, lawyer Kalman Ruttkay, a landowner, but by then already without property, since the communists had taken it from him, also lay on a shelf among books for a long time. His wife was a relatively young, beautiful widow with Hungarian-Romanian background around whom, despite her large aquiline nose and gender-dominant face, the "good guys" were still circling. However, when someone came to visit them, her daughter, Tibor's mother, immediately lit a candle by the library to "smoke him out" of there.

However, life went on and so she too found herself in an urn, for now in the hallway at Eva's, whose whole life was connected to the cemetery. She considered the dust in the urn to be a part of life, especially since she and Tibor's mother were somehow close. While Imro had wondered all his life how he could go from being a peasant from the east to becoming a squire of Turiec, when he came to them in Turiec, the most beautiful region in central Slovakia, Ruttkay was already a squire. Imro was accepted even without any property, Kalman's property was first taken away in order to make him his equal.

And so the urn with his mother's dust probably lay somewhere on a shelf in their apartment for a long time and perhaps it was eventually sold with the apartment after the death of Tibor's father, whom she married twice. The second time, because of the train fare[7]. What is certain is that she didn't take anything with her to the afterlife, just like everyone else.

---

7 A pass that allows you to get free dough.

She waited for him at the door in the hallway that adjoined the kitchen, where she usually smoked. He never told her where he was or when he would return. From the rustling behind the door, the length of time he spent looking for keys and unlocking the lock, she knew in what condition he was returning and was ready with the appropriate speech, which ended for him when he fell asleep and for her when she noticed that he was asleep.

This time she waited for him at Eva's. They sat at the kitchen table, Tibor read Poltvin aloud, which she had brought from work, and during breaks he went to pour vodka into the refrigerator that was right behind him.

He also drank when his girlfriend flew away. He rushed to the airport two hundred kilometers after her, but he didn't make it to the plane. At the gas station on the way back, he bought a reasonably spicy Debrecen baguette with ham, cheese and fresh onions, but he found a demijohn of her parents' homemade wine in the trunk, so he tasted it on the way back. About fifteen kilometers from home, the police stopped him to tell him that his light was out. But when they noticed that the driver could not speak, let alone get out of the car, they gave him a blow job. The result was the same as Rudolf's number, and while everyone was surprised that he was still alive, he called Eva to come get his car.

She found him at the police station, accompanied by two police officers. He was smoking his last cigarette, because everything else had already been taken from him, and he must have asked one of the police officers for it too. There was no time for long conversations, she took the car key and, looking at her friend leaving with a police escort, said goodbye.

His drinking was an obstacle for Eva. Imro drank enough to make her need another man in her life with this hobby, although it would probably turn out much better than with her husband. At the same time, she knew that as long as she was around Tibor, he would never find a girlfriend. She had to leave so that they could be free.

She found the car blushing at the rest stop. With one jolt, the one with which strong women are said to kill pigs, she placed the bumper in its original place, moved her seat, adjusted the mirrors, and then on the passenger seat she found an untouched Debrecen baguette with ham and cheese, but now with the onion raised. She parked the car in front of the house, threw the keys in the postbox, and waited.

Although he was ashamed, not for drinking, but for being caught and having to sleep at the police station, after a few days he called her to help him arrange a psychologist for new driving tests. She decided to call her former classmate, who was the sister of their mutual friend Bruno. Tibor gave her a phone to call from, but she was not allowed to say what the number was for. Everything went smoothly until Bruno asked if the number he was calling from was Eva's, because he had it saved as Tibor's.

She also drove him to the regional prosecutor's office and had no idea that one day she would also go through those police officers, investigations and courts, but alone. Her husband had only said one wise thing in his life, the bad guys band together, the good guys stay alone. And he consistently tried to make sure she was truly alone during those difficult times. He contacted her friends, wrote them messages, went to her work, but not to arrange a job, but to deprive Eva of her work. Without a job and without any income, she would be an easy victim when he started blackmailing her and suing her for the child. He went to kindergarten, everywhere one can imagine and especially where one cannot even imagine, because he had enough time. When he was "getting everything done", he ended up with the Jehovah's Witnesses. He managed to find a group of people, friends, kindred spirits, who stood by him, and who had a common enemy - Eva, who would never allow her child to become part of any sect.

She was proud and adamant, she was aware that even if they took everything from her, even if she drank water from a puddle, no one would take her daughter! She gave him a choice - either the Jehovah's Witnesses or her family. He chose.

When a tower collapses, not just one floor falls. A struggle began that lasted for many years and cost a lot of time, fear, negative emotions and, last but not least, resources. Eva lost her job from day to day. She did not take the excursions that she had promised herself she would never accompany, they humiliated her in other ways, made her fold envelopes for a candidate in the next election period and even came to check on her. When everything was decided and they called her to come and sign something, she painted her nails for the last time, waited for her nail polish to dry and went to get her resignation. The same person who fired her was also fired a few months later. The purges began, similar to those under the bolsheviks but this time they were also firing former informers, and somehow they caught their eye, her colleague Milan from the office. Where is she now listening to Green wave, drinking coffee and shuffling her feet? Does he have anywhere to make phone calls?

When she was at work for the last time to run errands, she put on a white leather coat from her golden age, when she worked in a completely different place and earned much more. She still doesn't know why, but her boss and former classmate in one person came to take a picture of her and praised her for it. She advised him that they gave out such coats at the employment office. Perhaps it was useful advice, because he was soon fired too, but whether he managed to take part in the campaign with white leather coats, Eva will probably never know.

At that time, she painted a portrait of A. S. Pushkin. She called it Pushkin-carnival and, with a sad dedication as a farewell, left it on Tibor's doorman at work. Although she didn't realize it, it was her farewell gesture before the arrival of liquidating events in her life, which she had never dreamed of even in her worst dreams. He was pleased, but in disbelief he threw her message in the trash. She was left alone for good.

She continued to take her daughter to kindergarten, waiting for her in the car. At first, she stopped by her friend Tibor's theater, but when she saw that she was no longer very welcome there, she stopped going there.

She tried all the time so that her daughter wouldn't notice anything, to protect her, so that she wouldn't hear anything, so that she could continue living her childhood regardless of what was happening in her mother's life. She didn't say anything to her, even though she felt it. Once she went to pick her up a little early, the children were outside in the yard and her daughter was screaming at her mother under the windows of Eva's former work. She remembered it for a long time afterwards, and Eva tried to explain to her that she couldn't wave to her from the window... she didn't tell her that she didn't work there anymore until much later.

*

She paid for her trip to the children's corner with the kindergarten, but her father forbade her from attending. He said he would call the police on her when she got there. She came, but when she saw him in the ball pool, she felt sick and had to leave so as not to throw him up along with the balls. The teacher said something else to her, but she didn't notice it anymore. She sat down on a bench outside and waited again. It was a period of endless waiting for everything, but only the most patient could win in the game of time...

Her husband took his daughter from the kindergarten, although by that time she had already been entrusted to Eva by a preliminary court order, and he didn't bother to bring her back the next day either. No one knew where he had gone, but he went to check her attendance at the kindergarten all the more consistently. His impudence and aggression were gaining intensity, supported and fed by the sect and nonsense with which he tried to infect Eva when he interpreted the theory that hell does not exist, which was probably an argument for why they could do whatever they wanted, but the scythe hit a stone… Eva did not need to listen to her husband's instructions, nor to any of his whisperers, Eva's advisor was her own conscience.

During the divorce, she was reproached for being unadaptable. For the first time, she was proud of this trait of hers, inherited from Imro, all the more so because it came from the mouth of the other party, who had been trying to sink her from the beginning. Katarina was for her the best defender of the other party, who looked exactly like what she did. Her head would need to be replaced, not plastic and jaw surgery.

*

All three were invited to a wedding in Poland. However, it was clear to Eva that she would not go anywhere with her husband. None of her acquaintances would listen to his nonsense that he liked to spread around him so much. Only once did she let him go to the theater with her friends. Kamil sat next to her then, saying nothing, just listening and looking at him. Eva knew that for him it was a kind of meditation and psychological exercise, for her husband it was just another exhibition. When his monologue was over, Kamil asked Eva to go for a walk with him. They walked through the most beautiful part of the city that they both loved. They did not talk. Eva knew why Kamil had called her and he knew that she knew it.

*

When she came to get her things, he said they weren't going anywhere, that he would call the police and that she wouldn't get across the border. When she started putting things in the suitcase, he grabbed her, started cursing her like a pig and strangling her. She lay on the ground in shock and pain. She was determined! She still doesn't know what she had packed in the suitcase, but when she was leaving with him, he tore it out of her and said he wasn't taking the suitcase because it wasn't hers. It was the suitcase he had bought for her. Instead, he gave her some old suitcase of his. With the last bit of strength, she threw the suitcase in the direction it had come from and left.

Although she kept putting it off, saving the situation and letting the scum pour on her head endlessly, it was clear to her that she had to leave. She moved to a cottage alone with her child. However, when she went to get her things this time, she parked further away from the apartment and waited in the car for her husband to leave the apartment. He went to Jehovah's Witnesses meetings, it was clear that it wouldn't last long. She knew about it, because he also took his daughter there a few times. However, when she found out that Jehovah's Witnesses were giving her some medication, she definitely canceled it.

Her husband was helped by her now former friends, who also moved him and gave him accommodation. Long after that, even though he no longer lived there, he still paid them "out of gratitude", although he had trouble paying her and the child even a single euro extra. Eva, who had bought everything for their shared apartment, took only the washing machine and duvets, leaving everything else to him.

Fate brought her to Bratislava, where she found a lawyer. Both were in the same situation. His half-brother had fabricated a trial against him because of his inheritance, which hung over him like a sword of Damocles. It was only a matter of time before the investigation would be completed and he, as the "boss of anti-social contraband", would be convicted. At every meeting, a special intervention unit was always present, watching his every move. However, Eva was convinced that only he could win her case, because none of the lawyers at the district court had experienced what he had. Socially, it was a handicap for him, but in the case of her case, it was a great asset.

After the incident in their apartment, a criminal complaint was filed against her husband, which began an investigation. In the meantime, he had already been in contact with his classmate and also a lawyer in one person, who filed a lawsuit against Eva. They began to sue for their daughter, while her husband was convinced and spread the word around town that he was in divorce proceedings, which Eva had started about ten years later, when she finally decided to get rid of that invisible bond, that meaningless promise, and that nut that strangled her, tied her hands, locked her in isolation from the whole world, a bond that sucked all the life-giving strength and energy out of her.

Eva and her family often heard threats that his lawyer knew the judge, that she would show Eva, and so on. She showed. She whistled hysterically, threw her arms around, rattled her kitschy beads, which she finally took off affectedly during the indictment, and for one variety show, which Eva no longer felt like attending, she put on a skirt the size of a belt, which none of the eyewitnesses present will easily forget for a long time. It didn't help. Although they had their own psychologist, who worked diligently on behalf of Jehovah's Witnesses' interests and made a very good living thanks to this service on behalf of the needs of the black factory with children, it didn't help. The deal with Eva's child didn't work out. The entry in the file said - maladaptive.

When her husband started taking the child and going to kindergarten more and more often, because the order from the Jehovah's Witnesses to "get a child" was an order for a mindless machine like him, she slowly started moving to Bratislava. A bribed district court judge gave her exactly three days to find a job, a kindergarten for the child, and accommodation in the hope that she would not succeed. She succeeded. To this day, she considers it a miracle, but also an impulse that it really was meant to be. In three days, with their tongues hanging out, they flew over Bratislava fifteen times, founded a company, found a place for the child in a state kindergarten, and Eva moved to safety.

After about a week in Bratislava, she threw the Canadian nut from the hardware store in the trash. Although she had almost no income, every other week she had to take her daughter to "meetings" with her father to tell him that she was not going anywhere with him.

His malice went so far that during another visit to a kindergarten in Bratislava, where he was brought again by her former friends, he entered the classroom among the children, did not bring her daughter a banana or an apple, but demanded attendance. The elderly teacher, accustomed to such outbursts, cold-bloodedly chased him out to the kindergarten gates. He did not give up and that same day sent an anonymous letter to Eva's father asking him not to give her money because she had started a company and that meant she had money. She did not. Friends and acquaintances brought and sent her food, homemade preserves, lard with the words "you will eat this when you have nothing", bananas in chocolate and biscuits for her daughter, everything from the table and whenever possible.

While Eva's father was alive, her mother had to give her money for rent from time to time. She usually withdrew them from a cash machine because she didn't have such a large amount on her and she did it very reluctantly. Before, they had shared access to their father's account, she had the card and Eva knew the password. Later, her mother took everything and then threw money at her on the street, which Eva had to collect in front of everyone so that she would have a place to live and, above all, what to pay for the next month. She was a hunted animal by society and the judiciary, which only watched when the mother made a mistake, when she failed.

Her husband had no creative thinking, but his imagination knew no bounds when it came to ways to harm someone. Eva always said that if she wanted to destroy someone, she would introduce them to her husband and he would do the rest. He just took all the important documents from Eva, such as receipts for her half-sisters' payments from their father's house, without which they had to pay them again, permanent resident cards in Canada that had lost their validity, and the like. He probably sent those documents directly to them, because otherwise they would know that she had no way to defend herself in court when they sued her in court and demanded a re-payment from her father's property.

When they say that she was a swindler, it was doubly true of Eva's sisters. They teased her father during his life, and they teased him after his death. He considered his eldest daughter a partner and liked to spend time talking to her. He couldn't stand the middle one, for reasons that were previously inexplicable to Eva. Later she understood why. Too late.

She had a boyfriend from the High Tatras. Her father liked him. He always said how happy he was to come because Eva always cooked and cleaned. But one day she returned from the Tatras earlier than usual. She found messages on her boyfriend's phone from her middle sister's daughter, Eva's niece. While she was working abroad, she sent her daughter to him. It broke her, and then she sent a message to her classmate, as a response to his unfinished dialogue from years ago, which he no longer remembered at the wedding, with the text "let's get married". The answer came immediately - "I work on Saturday". And so began the dramatic part of Eva's life, which sometimes resembled more a variety show, other times a farce.

Her husband, however, was so proud of his performances that he recorded everything, in case Hollywood filmmakers were interested. However, it can be said with a clear conscience that as an actor he was too affected and worthless. However much he wanted to harm, it was only naive attempts and evidence of his wretchedness that definitively confirmed to Eva that she would never go anywhere on this path and with this man. Although he had a collection of cash registers and recordings, he did not have a single photo of his family together.

One night before they left for Bratislava, he called the police. Saying that they weren't going anywhere, he blocked her car door and comically tried to turn on the recording on his mobile phone for a few tens of seconds, maybe a minute. Her mother then hid again in the bathroom or the pantry, and her blind father with a cane went to talk to the officers. Eva waited for the police to release her, because there was no reason to detain her, but it was too late and she still had two hundred kilometers ahead of her. On the way, she tried to call Tibor one last time to tell him what had happened, so that she could at least tell someone what had happened, but it didn't work, he didn't have time for her anymore, not even a word. He wasn't there for her anymore. So she turned on the radio and listened to the redactor talking to someone, and that someone was reading the Bible. She turned it off and although she had previously respected that important text, after several lectures by her husband in the Jehovah's Witness spirit, she definitely developed an aversion to it. The Jehovah's Witness leaflets that he left in their mailbox wouldn't even burn.

*

Eva's father's health condition continued to deteriorate. At first, her mother would call her and ask what to give him to eat, because he was no longer taking anything. They bought vitamins, after which his hair started to grow even on his bald spot, where he had none his whole life. The only thing he ate was bryndza[8]. After each stay in the hospital, he had to be put back on his feet again and again. He still felt anxious. His world was dark, both during the day and at night.

*

It was Saturday. Autumn. The days were shorter. It was long past visiting hours at the hospital. But something was pulling Eva there. She desperately needed to see her father. She walked through the sad

---

8 A dairy product, similar to cheese.

and quiet area. Everything was dark and gray. She climbed the stairs to the ward, but the hallway door was closed. She didn't try the handle. She turned and ran down the stairs. She stopped. She went back. She pushed the door open without any problems.

Her father's bed was right behind the door. It was dark. She stood by her father's bed and cried. He wasn't sleeping.

- Are you here? - he asked.

- Yes, dad.

- Are you driving?

- Yes.

- Take me home, - he begged.

She wanted to do it. She wanted to stop what was coming, but she couldn't. He was just a shell that would burst if someone grabbed him. She stroked his hand in tears and left again in the dark.

They also slept with their daughter at the cottage. In the morning, mother's phone rang. Eva would never do that, to take someone else's call, but her mother was in the bathroom and picked it up. They were calling from the hospital. Her father died during the night. Eva refused an autopsy. He suffered unbearable pain until the last moment, she didn't want to bother him anymore after his death.

Eva´s mother was going to go to the hospital to see him. When Eva told her that they had just called from the hospital, that they didn't have to anymore, they almost fought. Her mother started spouting nonsense at her again, as she had done all her life, but now the man who had protected her from her outbursts was no longer there. But she needed to show her importance, so she called the hospital and ordered an autopsy.

They didn't speak to each other until the notary's summons. Her mother had lived her whole life only for the old or the dead. She wasn't interested in living. She spent whole days in the cemetery. She had all her old friends there. She visited them, talked to them, and even though her home was unbearably messy, she regularly criticized the cemetery management for the occasional uncut grass or fallen branch.

Eva did not come back until the day of the funeral. Her father had prepared the grave and the tombstone in advance. He had also taken his older daughters to it if they wanted to bring him flowers. However, Eva was convinced that if it was not flowing from his side, it would not drip from theirs either. There was no longer any motivation or reason for visits. The relationships that her father had built his whole life had been definitively severed.

It was a big funeral. Eva was incredibly sad. She could not go to the coffin, she could only look from afar at the person closest to her who was leaving somewhere. She did not notice anyone that day. She could barely distinguish voices. The room was stuffy and then she remembered the unnecessary autopsy and felt sick. She had to sit down.

She realized that she had not seen anyone from her father's sister's side, they probably had not been informed. She had died so suddenly, shortly after her grandfather and Ulyka. Actually, Ulyka, the grandfather's second wife, died first. Eva had never liked her. She didn't feel comfortable there when her father left her with them, even though she gave her sugar, she remembers that.

When the ceremony was over, they carried the coffin into the car and the crowd headed for the grave.

- Go after the coffin!

She heard a voice from behind her and felt a hand on her shoulder. She was her father's cousin. She was the closest to him in the whole family. They had grown up together when his mother died. She ironed his shirts when he went to school, she ironed them even after he got divorced, she ironed them even when he got married a second time. Eva lived with her when she went to college. She taught her everything her mother was supposed to teach her. That day, and no other day, she couldn't talk to Eva, because her older sisters had brought her there, and from the conversations in the car she could guess how it would all turn out. That sentence was the last Eva ever heard from her. The hand on her shoulder disappeared into the crowd that was walking behind her. She obeyed and followed the coffin, even though her knees were giving way, she couldn't see or hear anything that was happening around her.

The coffin was lowered on ropes into the grave that her father had prepared, in the place where he wanted to lie. She was terribly sad! She cried and through her tears she couldn't see anyone, she just felt her unbearable grief. Her daughter stood by her. She didn't know where the others were. They were no longer in her life.

Her college classmate spoke for the city. They lived next to each other in the dormitory, they traveled to school together every Sunday by train. She didn't listen to what he was saying, she just squeezed his hand tightly with both hands, which he gave her as a sign of condolences.

She stood there for a long time and cried. She said goodbye to her father for a long time. She didn't want to believe that she wouldn't hear from him anymore, that she wouldn't see him anymore. When her mother called her from his phone, she didn't pick up. She didn't want to hear her there, but her father!

The father decided where he would be buried and that could not be changed, but he also decided where he would have his funeral and his wife changed that. She threw a funeral at a hotel, for over a hundred people, but she forgot to invite them there. Eva didn't know where it would be either, but she knew the local petty-bourgeois conditions and instinct led her to the right place. Her mother and about three other people sat on one side, Eva on the other, but closer to her father's older daughters.

Her older sister's daughter was forced by her mother to apologize to Eva. She did so as they were leaving, but very theatrically. When everyone was leaving, she ran away, knocked her glasses off her nose and hit Eva. Was she apologizing for hitting her or for going to see her boyfriend?

Eva's mother began a new, happy life that day. She got rid of her husband, her daughter and her granddaughter. She became a famous and wealthy widow.

Eva's husband didn't even bother to send her a text message to express his condolences. Her father was not his father-in-law, and his Jehovah's Witness career also prevented him from doing so. Only a few months later, when his mother called her, she asked in the middle of the conversation how her father was doing. Eva thought for a moment that he was joking, for a moment she wanted to hang up the phone, and only when she took a breath did she coldly and sternly say that he was no longer there.

*

The manipulated candidate for the watchtower guard, however, worked tirelessly. He spent whole days looking at the file that statistician Etelka did not even want to show her lawyer. He wrote out criminal charges against Eva and presented as evidence the recordings of the child, which Eva refused to listen to during interrogations. However, Etelka heroically managed to capture the domestic violence conviction from the prosecutor's office and it ended up in the drawer of the wrinkled, crooked and toothy Katarina as proof of the quality work of the district court in the name of "justice". Perhaps one day she will use it to blackmail her client to finally pay her for her devoted services. In order to hide his psychological problems, Eva's husband tried, of course with the help of his closest brothers and sisters, to get Eva, if not to a mental institution, then at least to convince her that she could not take care of her daughter because she was not well. Where his level of order was, it was not determined, but what is certain is that he was not "in order", after all, who would think of checking an herbal solution from a pharmacy intended for gums?! Who would turn a mother and child into hunted animals?!

The fact is that the more pressure he created, the more resistance he encountered. He did not care about the child at all, he would have lost it anyway. It would probably be somewhere with the Jehovah's Witnesses, just like Eva's money, which is no longer talked about at all today. It is time-barred and the culprit claims that he does not remember anything. He probably does not even remember the child and consistently adheres to Jehovah's ideas, according to which the child does not have birthdays, name days, Christmas, or other holidays, and instead of the prestigious private school in the capital that Eva arranged for her, she probably attends a rural school, because the money he pays her covers exactly such a life.

When Eva's daughter went on mandatory trips with her father, Eva would wait for her in the car. It was cold, the village under the High Fatra was already freezing, everything was freezing for Eva. She could no longer go to the cottage and she could not afford to sit in the car that had been started. He never brought his daughter on time, but the opposite case, that is, that Eva would do something similar, was more than excluded. Once, when she returned, she told Eva that some lady was helping him. Eva did not know who she was for a long time, until one day they met a social worker and then her child finished her sentence - that was the lady who was helping him. Yes, she was helping him, against the interests of the child, who has lived in Bratislava for ten years, but the social welfare office that is in charge of him is not there. The assistant of the Ombudsman for Children's Rights wrote to her at the time that she did not know what she was talking about when she sent her the documentation from the lawyer and that was the end of the matter.

They tried to solve it through the embassy when she worked for a foreign institute, to no avail. For Eva, she had no company, no offices, no spreadsheets, and so she was unsolvable, almost transparent.

She lost her job again and again, or her job situation was so bad that she left on her own. She lost friends, people who helped her one day, were no longer in her life the next day for unknown reasons. The more often it happened to her, the less she reacted to it. She watched it only as a story about someone she could not influence, because any intervention or attempt to change was just a waste of money she did not have.

At that time, she also lost her lawyer. The long-running case of his lawsuit was coming to an end. The summons for the final hearing came. Eva was convinced that she would hear from him after two hours. He did not answer after two or three. His phone was turned off. She didn't want to admit that fate had played such a trick on her. But the truth was that he had been convicted and imprisoned that day. He had written to her from prison, asking her to save his personal belongings that could still be saved before his friends, who were also now exes, stole them. She had managed to do some things, but she hadn't managed to do some things. She met one of them wearing her lawyer's sweater.

She gathered everything she needed, took the box with the family jewels with her, and put it in the closet as she found it. But she had to look for a lawyer again. There are plenty of lawyers, but one who would go outside Bratislava to hear the hearings in a rigged dispute with Jehovah's Witnesses, where the child's father is running for the position of Watchtower guard... there was only one, and he was a bit closed off at the time. No one knew how long he would be there. No one knew what was going on behind the scenes of the district court, which was guarded by Etelka, and the Bible on the shelf behind her, a gift from Eva's husband. Like a cat with kittens, Eva walked around the law offices with the file until she found a seemingly neutral ground where she would feel somehow safe. The young girls, law graduates, did not know what they were getting into and, to tell the truth, did not believe in a victorious ending. The logic of the whole thing was quite different from victorious. However, their task was not to resolve anything fundamental, Eva clearly told them to keep the dispute in the state it was in, because she believed that one day her lawyer would return and fate would arrange it so that it would be on time.

She was quite surprised when various people from prison came to see her. Suddenly, they found themselves at the door, without ringing the bell, and Eva just smiled, because she knew that there was no door they could not open. They brought her gifts, greetings, flowers, she received letters, even from a painter who was imprisoned for making copies of famous paintings, she received two paintings that he had painted in prison. Her lawyer worked there too, helping those whom no one wanted to help, from whom everyone was pulling their hands away, just like from him or from Eva with the child.

She managed to find a job in a publishing house near where they lived. She was very happy, even though the money she received there was only enough for rent. At first, she was happy that after a long time she had a job she enjoyed again and her daughter also started going to school. Everything seemed to fall into place.

During one of the last phone calls, her husband's mother announced the great news that her precious son was no longer in Slovakia. He was at the time with his brother, who had two sons, whom he was taking care of alone. Eva's husband needed to comment on their upbringing, and that's when their mother called and asked him how many children he had raised in his life? They adopted the child from his first marriage right at the beginning, and he had been trying to get a second child for a few years. That's when he decided to return to Canada in a short time.

Of course, it wasn't without a "farewell" incident, when the village experienced a variety show on such a scale that the child couldn't even breathe into the phone to tell her what had happened.

At that time, Eva was visiting the children with whom she was rehearsing her original performance. Every Friday she flew a four hundred kilometer round trip. Her daughter had been taken to dance school for the time being, and she returned for her at six o'clock sharp. She was never late! The day her husband left, the children had their first performance. She picked up her daughter from school and they went to the performance together. As if she had suspected, he came to the school for an inspection that very day and, with his exaggerated self-confidence, supported by the Jehovah's Witness program of chosenness, headed straight for the principal's office. It must have been interesting, because the child went to a private language school and even with her overactive imagination, Eva could hardly imagine him talking to anyone there. In her life, she had only heard him swear in a foreign language.

*

One day, like every day, while she was at work, her phone rang. The name of her old lawyer appeared on the display. It was the first thing she had been genuinely happy about in a long time. Especially the fact that he was alive at all. It was a miracle that he had survived the prison diet with celiac disease and a transplanted stomach, and the second thing was that he was calling her from the same number he had, as if nothing had happened in the meantime. She left the office and went to make a phone call outside on the stairs so that her colleagues wouldn't hear her, because the doors to all the offices were always open. It was really strange when she saw the same old, familiar number. They always talked in codes that only they understood, because their phones had long been tapped. Even Eva had a tapped phone. She subconsciously felt during the conversation that she wasn't alone with the person she was calling. Finally, she took the card out of her phone and left it on the shelf. When she wanted to cancel the number, the employee told her that the number was still in use.

By canceling the number, phone calls to her husband's relatives also ended, especially his mother, who had never done anything for Eva, except to inform her about her trips to America when Eva couldn't even afford to eat. With the cancellation of the number, an era in Eva's life ended, which left along with the list of numbers on the card.

Her husband was able to arrange something for her, unfortunately, nothing useful. An oversized police woman helped him with the criminal complaint. However, there was nothing from either the recordings or the report, and the policewoman also had false hopes, in women like her he only aroused hope, but that never turned into and never had a chance to turn into an opportunity. Eva could have handed out instructions for use if anyone was interested, but no one approached her, so she was just amused from afar by the naivety of those around her, and her husband was furious because he had never seen her jealous. If she was ever jealous, it certainly wasn't of him and the ladies around him, he didn't have a discerning taste for that.

That same day, she handed over to her lawyer a box of family jewels that he had ordered her to take from his then-rented apartment. When they closed it, his former friends had stolen everything from him, but he had made a point of emphasizing that nothing was missing from the box. It was obvious to Eva that she wouldn't touch something that didn't belong to her. It hadn't even occurred to her. Maybe she was just a little embarrassed that he would think such a thing, but the environment he had just returned from had probably prepared him for this way of thinking.

She was sorry, but even though she had arranged a visit to the prison, she could not go to see him. He brought her gifts, albeit small, symbolic ones, but he brought gifts from prison for Eva and her daughter!

Before their last hearing at the district court, he admitted to her that he did not know what would happen. He had something prepared, but no one knew how things would turn out. He managed to reconstruct the file from the prosecutor's office, which was faithfully kept by the statistician Etelka according to instructions and handed over to the opposing side, only to end up forgotten in the drawer of the toothy lawyer Katka. The court also managed to present a photo of the "grieving" father from a celebration with friends, who in this way was probably "grieving" for his daughter, whom, according to his lawyer, he could not reach. She did not mention that she was rejecting him.

Eva and her daughter won this battle, but they still haven't won the fight for their own, free, and fulfilling life in this world.

*

Their paths diverged at the end of the trial. It was necessary to move on. After some time, however, they met in a department store. She would not have noticed him if he had not spoken to her. It was a very short and pleasant meeting, and Eva left with the feeling that they had parted ways on good terms.

*

The pandemic broke out. Eva's boss was on vacation with his girlfriend, who was half a century younger. One of four, for whom we had to work hard, because her love of money was stronger than the world's epidemic measures.

He had no idea what was going on in Bratislava. His employees had to go to work, which they could easily do from home. Eva had been upset with him for a long time. He always chose someone, and now it was her turn. She was worried about her daughter, about her health, so she decided to leave alone. As soon as he returned from vacation, she left his keys at the reception and left without a word. He allegedly asked about her, calling everyone into the office one by one, but to no avail, they were unanimous in not telling him what he wanted to hear. Eva did not return, and his expensive vacations, and especially their frequency, completely ruined him and destroyed the company.

*

Eva had bought a plot of land in the south. She managed to sell it at the beginning of the year, so she could leave her job, where mothers with small children were not counted.

When all the epidemic restrictions were imposed, when life on the planet stopped, she would go to the store every now and then in big, yellow, rubber gloves. She would leave her purchases at the door of their old town apartment and then she and her daughter would wait to get to the chocolate as quickly as possible.

When humanity was let out a little for the summer, the restrictions were relaxed, they loaded their things into the car and headed south again. Along the way, she stopped for coffee with her loved ones, who always helped her, supported her and sent her all their homemade goodies.

Eva always wrote, she was always where something was happening, but when she got married, she was left in a kind of isolation. Suddenly she couldn't do what she used to do, she didn't feel useful and it was killing her psychologically. Janko, Eva's long-time very good friend, knew about it, although she didn't tell him, and he often wrote to her. He sent her texts for correction so that she could give him her opinion, although it wasn't as important to him as it was to her.

In her daughter's kindergarten, she met the grandfather of one of her classmates. He met Eva's father and often witnessed her husband's antics at the kindergarten, when he walked around like a wolf around a flock of sheep, who thinks that they are all his and will obey him, and when he is hungry, they will jump on his plate.

The man called her every weekend and told her what was new,

to keep her alive, because he was the only person who called the non-existent Eva. He would call a hundred times if she didn't answer, just to get through to hold her. He had bunnies, they got one from him when they still lived at the cottage. Together with her daughter, they would go and pick the most beautiful dandelion leaves in the whole village. But when they finally had to leave, the bunny stayed in the freezer, and it's probably still there today, because the new owner of the cottage won't put up with it. At that time, Eva had to do many things that she would never do under normal circumstances. She had to leave everything that was dear and close to her. She had to leave the dog that her mother didn't care for at all and the neighbor promised her that she would bring him food from work. She had to leave the house she grew up in. She had to leave the house her daughter grew up in. To live and survive in makeshift homes. Everything she dreamed of was gone.

*

She was leaving again. The car was fully loaded, she had no idea it could fit so much, and in the middle of it all was her daughter. They went south again. They went there for Christmas so they wouldn't be alone and for the summer when her daughter was on vacation. It was paradise for her and for a while Eva felt like a child was living her real childhood, outside, in the garden, among animals and with her friends. There she developed values, nice emotions that were supposed to be overshadowed by interrogations and court battles.

But Simona already had other plans and Tatiana was responsible for implementing her plans; if she couldn't achieve something, she would complain and seek help from Vinco. Eva didn't come "home" anymore. The collection of clothes for her child had also been stopped. They were given a room on the top floor of the house, they would go there to hide so they wouldn't get in the way. If Simona wasn't there, Tatiana's phone rang with instructions right away in the morning, and then a brief message came to Eva, with the text - When are you leaving?

Where she was supposed to go during the pandemic, without a job and without income with a school-age child, Eva had no idea at all.

When something was eaten, Eva disappeared so that she wouldn't be blamed and so that the child would have more left. She tried to help, cleaned the cows, baked a cake, learned how to make korbaciky[9]. Nothing was good. The cheese that could have been saved by making korbaciky was thrown away, just so as not to make a mess that inevitably arises with every job. Before Eva usually went to clean the cows, Tatiana quickly cleaned, before Eva got there, she didn't say anything to her, sat down in a garden chair overlooking the barns and was happy to see Eva walking around the cleaned barns with cows ready to go to pasture.

Eva didn't have money for a hairdresser, so she asked Simona to help her dye her hair. She couldn't. Eva dyed it herself, but Simona came to the bathroom to remind her not to get anything dirty, because ammonia-free dye couldn't be washed off. The bathroom was very old, the rotten and damp-swollen wooden door never closed, there was only a bathtub and a mirror. No, Eva didn't get anything dirty, but Simona didn't give up, and when she was done, she came to check how she had dyed her hair.

This cold war lasted the whole summer, its intensity gradually escalating. Although Eva tried not to react to the nonsense she regularly encountered and which crushed her spirit screaming for development, she had to "suck it up" to the bottom. The escape from this situation was a contact in the capital, the prospects of cooperation for Eva and especially the possibility of a school for her daughter and the associated definitive departure. But that was preceded by the last drop in the glass.

Simona called her to have a beer together. Simona's seemingly

---

9 Cheese product.

calm monologue began. They were sitting in the yard. Simona was talking, Eva was silent, and Tatiana was running around them, but Eva, sitting with her back to her, couldn't see her. Her daughter was playing opposite her, wanting to see her. Suddenly Tatiana screamed. She caught hold of a word from the monologue.

The day before, they had been in town with them, and while Tatiana and Vinco were packing their things, Eva and her daughter were walking around and, as always, taking pictures of colorful goats, sheep, and shepherds returning up the street from the pasture. But Tatiana started shouting something about boarding houses, about Simona's lies, and suddenly a tin baking dish flew right past Eva's head, followed by an entire wicker garden chair. Simona, however, blamed Eva because she needed her there a lot and told them to leave when they were putting her mother in such a state. Eva didn't have time to say anything the whole time, and she didn't say anything after that either. She took the child by the hand and headed for the mountain. They couldn't leave so quickly, they had unloaded all their belongings, she wouldn't have had time to load them into the car, otherwise they would have left forever that evening, which was probably planned in Simona's script.

On the way up the street to the valley, they met an unsuspecting Vinco in a friendly conversation with the neighbors. It was evening, it was getting dark, and Eva had no idea where they would sleep, she didn't know what to tell her daughter. They walked up through the village, which was already dark. They had nothing. As they were, in flip-flops, shorts, and T-shirts, they climbed higher and higher. Eva knew that they had to sleep under a roof, so she headed for the mill that they both knew.

The old water mill sheltered them. The daughter knew where the key was, she often played there when something was being done up there, around it. Usually, potatoes were planted there, which were either being mowed, hoeed, watered, or dug up. Now they were just dozing there and listening to the murmur of the stream. It was quiet, and until it got completely dark, Eva sat by the door. She needed to breathe.

There was only one room in the mill with a large mill wheel, tools, and a bed made of a few planks, covered with a sheet. They lay down. When the cold from the river and the mountain began to seep through the planks into the room, their daughter brought a coat and they covered themselves with it. Until morning they listened to the murmur of the stream and the squeaking of mice, who were looking for seeds and crumbs and giving each other signals, instead of going to bed. Everything creaked, cracked, decomposed, came into being and disappeared, living its own life as if it were not there. In the morning, when all the sounds tired them, they fell asleep.

Down in the village, life was already in full swing, the sun was only slowly making its way into the mountain when they returned, frozen. Eva had an important meeting that day, they had to hurry. She was taking her daughter with her, because she didn't want to leave her in such an environment. They walked through the back yard, because Eva wasn't sure if the gate in front would be open. She went to change. She had long since given up on the idea of washing herself. Her daughter was waiting for her in the yard.

On the way to the room, Simona caught up with her like a fury. Vinco was talking to his daughter, and Tatiana was lost, as she always was when something important was being resolved. She was lost in the same way as Eva's mother or Eva's husband, when they felt guilty and afraid at the same time.

-Where do you go at night with the child? - the question was heard among a number of other specific sounds, screams and hysterical expressions, which Eva now perceived only as the shrieks of chimpanzees echoing near the butterfly pavilion. She knew what she and Tatiana had done to Milos and promised herself that this would never happen to her and her daughter again.

Despite the nonsense she had to listen to while Simona stood in the doorway screaming, she managed to get dressed. Doing her hair, putting on makeup and drinking coffee would have been a bonus she hadn't counted on that morning. But she was happy that they would be gone for the whole day and that they would be fine.

Frozen and sleepless, they shivered in the car, in which Eva, in the middle of the hot summer, was heating up. The consul was already waiting for them in the city, and the great expedition to a new life could begin. Even though there was a pandemic and no one knew what would happen tomorrow, Eva, the only one, felt somehow freer that day than everyone else on the planet.

*

A few weeks later, they really left. Simona had been gone for several days. Eva didn't ask where she was, because she wouldn't have found out the truth from Tatiana anyway, and she didn't care anymore. She went to the post office to buy a highway stamp. The postwoman also knew that they were leaving and greeted her with the words:

- I was very pleased to meet you.

Eva was surprised, but only for a moment. She realized that in the village, everything is known before it happens. Tatiana was so happy that they were leaving that she must have told everyone, because aunt Kata from the cat house also brought them bananas for the trip. Nobody knew where they were going, nobody asked, she didn't tell anyone. Eva knew that she had nowhere to go back to, she had to keep going. So they set off for the capital.

Eva was still at the gate telling Tatiana that she had left some things with them that she couldn't take. As always, they said they would send them to her through a neighbor who drives a truck, or they said they would pick them up when they arrived for Christmas. They neither sent them, nor did they come to get them, nor did they respond to messages of various kinds. Another chapter of her life was definitively closed, scum, poured on her head, spilled over.

Sometimes before the holidays, a neighbor who liked Eva called her, but not because he had something to bring her, but because he asked about her, and Simona answered him with the question:

- Who is that?

From then on, she was definitely not without remorse.

*

In Sofia, Eva started teaching again and her daughter got into a good local school. For a while they went to school, for a while they were online like the rest of the world. They lived with a beautiful view of Vitosha. Eva would spend hours by the window looking at that natural monument, and in the evening she would wait for the lights that illuminated the mountain huts on top of the mountain. Suddenly she looked at the streets of Sofia with completely different eyes, at the people she met every day. She could talk to them and until a certain point they didn't even notice that she wasn't from there. She knew the language, knew the grammar, but she kept her strong accent well under control.

They spent the beautiful, sunny autumn walking in the parks, or sitting somewhere or walking around the city with hot chocolate, usually moving somewhere between pet stores where there were kittens or puppies. Sofia always knows how to surprise, and that's why Eva likes her.

With the money she received for lessons, they always went to buy something for school or some clothes, because the seasons were changing and her daughter had grown a lot.

Eva managed to get her old computer running in front of the

store, and although the course of the pandemic here was relatively calm and mild, the measures were taken and respected with reason, when the children stayed home, she found it very useful in her studies and Eva was able to continue translating the book she was working on at the time and teaching at the same time and preparing dictation for each lesson. Always a new continuation of the story. During this period, four books of stories were created. Every time she and her daughter went to the store, she asked her opinion on how it should continue. She taught girls about the same age as her and wanted it to be not only mandatory but also interesting for them.

Paradoxically, now they could go wherever they wanted. Although various binding measures were in effect, they went outside more than ever before. Eva was happy that her daughter was really happy. After a long time, they felt free. Eva promised herself that she would never let anyone lose that freedom again, unfortunately, she had to walk a thousand kilometers to find that lost feeling. It was as if her own time, which she had lost somewhere, had returned to her. She had to remember the taste of freedom. At that time, it tasted like cotton candy that they had bought in the park, it was pink, blue and very sweet.

They celebrated Christmas and New Year alone, but mostly the way they wanted. They modestly decorated their apartment, bought something good that they had been craving all year, but they didn't buy it to have something to look forward to. Eva certainly didn't bake. She only baked at home, back in the day, as a child. She had never baked since she had to move. She wanted to a couple of times, and she even bought a blender twice, but she always lost it. One blender, which she had freshly brought from the store, was given by her husband to Majchiatko, a lady for whom Eva wouldn't even buy a toothbrush. With the second blender, she was more careful and prudently signed the box - it didn't help, Eva's father gave it to a neighbor who came to clean for him and sometimes brought something sweet so that she had something to do with it. Here, somewhere, Eva's ambition to bake something in a kitchen whose contents she did not decide on ended. She remembers that for Christmas she bought her daughter a microscope that she wanted so much when they were walking around the store. She liked to look at macro objects in the sky and she already had a telescope for those, but she still needed a microscope for the micro ones.

New Year was beautiful, colorful and loud. After midnight, fireworks started to shoot, but they were as beautiful as they had ever seen. There were people in all the windows around, there were people outside, and where the fireworks went off, all eyes were on them. Suddenly they were kind of close. They stood by the window for a long time until the last fireworks went off. Up on Vitosha there was light and it seemed to Eva as if they were disturbing the mountain, but she stood there kindly and welcomed the new year with them.

Eva remembers the Christmas and New Year that she spent alone in Sofia at the boarding school. She bought a box of chocolates and oranges and studied, she had to defend her dissertation, which she was writing. Years later, history repeated itself, but instead of a dissertation, she was already writing fairy tales and had her first reader, critic, and co-author with her.

*

They invited them over for a visit during the holidays. Eva's longtime friend, through thick and thin, Maja, invited her to their home, there was no other way to go anyway. She had been to their house a hundred times before, normally she would have found it with her eyes closed, but now she circled, wandered, and went around, until she finally parked and walked.

She was never late anywhere if it depended on her, but now she felt that this was different, as if something was preventing them from finding a familiar alley, from waving under the window to have them open. It took an endless hour to find them. Under normal circumstances, Eva would have turned around long ago, but she appreciated the invitation and especially their friendship.

She had known their older daughter since she was a child. When she visited them as a student, they spoke Slovak and she thought her name was Ahoj[10]. The girls have grown up, only they are still here and that's how it will stay, while they walk the earthly path with the faith that something beautiful will remain after them, with the certainty of their wonderful daughters, for whom life is meaningful.

Although it was already dark when they left, they found the path to the car right away and were surprised at how easy it was to get there. On the way back, they didn't meet anyone. The streets were empty on the last day before the start of a new week, when everyone was walking their own paths immersed in everyday problems and challenges, someone might be changing jobs, someone might be trying their luck at a job interview.

Eva was preparing lunch for her daughter when the message rang. She had just finished maneuvering with a pot full of hot water. The message from Maja was on the display. She opened the entire text, which, despite its serious content, was written with deliberation and calmness. Her husband, a police officer in good shape who had been with them the whole time, had been in the hospital on life support for a week.

She didn't say anything to her daughter. She just quietly finished cooking lunch while she had online classes. Occasionally, she would discreetly grab her forehead and watch her closely for a few days. For the first time, she realized how close the invisible threat was. At the same time, she knew that under no circumstances should they give up. It was after two previous promises to herself that her daughter would never be a tool of some sect and a promise in the name of personal freedom, the third promise - to survive under all circumstances.

---

10   Ahoj means Hi in English.

But the numbers of infected people were rising and governments decided to close the borders again. But now they were on the other side and no one knew how long this situation would last. She felt the unswallowed lump in her throat again, her living space was narrowing again. She had to make a decision.

*

They were happy, but that feeling was temporary. What if, what if something happens? They are just dependent on each other, here and now, with no vision of a stable future.

Eva felt again that terrible uncertainty that had haunted her for years and regularly returned, strengthened by the responsibility for the child for whom she wanted only the best, but no matter what she did, there was no way to change it.

She didn't like to do it, but she decided. Before the border closed, they would leave. It was February and that was also the decision. Winters in Bulgaria are usually harsh and Eva didn't want another one. She was also afraid of the journey with a loaded car and a child. Some time ago, acquaintances with whom she had once been in Brno contacted her. They lived under the forest, they offered them accommodation. It was still not a job offer that would provide them with any security, but it was another short-term solution and support in uncertain times.

They lived in a part of Slovakia that Eva had never wanted to get to know. It was a forgotten corner of the world, but because circumstances had stopped the rest of the world from seeing it, it wasn't felt that way there.

For both of their acquaintances, it was a second marriage. A second chance at life to follow the same path. It didn't help. Andrea's first husband was a soldier. The second one did something different, but the military training, hysterical screaming, and thick stuffiness he spread around him could be cut. His first wife looked like Andrea.

Neither of them had any contact with the children from their first marriage. Together they had a son of about the same age as Eva's daughter. He grew up alone, with his parents in the forest, without peers, equal challenges, in social isolation that was supposed to protect him carefully.

The children did not go to school. The boy was homeschooled and Eva's daughter was in online school. The great English teacher was nowhere to be seen, but during her lessons he would often poke around for a light, and the screen would be covered by a plume of smoke so intense that it could be felt even in the room.

They were in an unheated room, in the forest, in the middle of winter, but they were glad to have some kind of roof over their heads and were grateful. There was no heating in their Bulgarian apartment either, but they didn't feel it there, and when necessary, they turned on the heater, even if only for a moment, to keep warm.

Their lives were adapting to the pandemic measures, but the days they lived under the mountain were almost the same, until a certain time. As they say, on the third day, both the fish and the guest start to stink. This thought kept coming to Eva, and she searched again for a solution. However, no matter how hard she tried and didn't want to live like that, she couldn't get a job, no one responded to her resume, although she felt like everyone had already read it. She couldn't even go to work as a cleaner, everything was closed, no one was at work and there was simply no garbage either.

She was demoted and undervalued. Although she had previously worked at the university, today she was sent to a social club when she applied for the job she had done before at the ministry, they laughed at her when she sent resumes to any vacancies, she was overqualified with two doctorates. Was there no place for her under the sun!?

She found a temporary solution when she remembered the phone call with her half-sister. Eva's mother kept complaining that she had to pay off her father's daughters. She wouldn't have had to if Eva's husband hadn't taken all the documents he had about her father's transfers. Imro wanted to do it quietly and intelligently, because he also relied on the intelligence of her sisters. Unsuccessfully. Intelligence was not found during the autopsy, their medical report would say. They asked again, and because Eva didn't believe it, she called her. Zuza confirmed it to her and that ended their conversation, and any contact.

Eva had one rule - she never returned anywhere. She endured a lot, let the scum pour on her head, but when it overflowed and she left, she never returned there again. She was sorry, but she knew that she would never return to her native region. She considered Bratislava a stopover before the border and these transfers as crisis solutions. So she decided to break the century-old silence and ask her mother for her share of the house left by her father. It was strange, but with only a little hesitation, which only Eva noticed in her voice, they agreed on some ridiculous amount, which, however, helped Eva a lot. For security reasons, although they were about two hundred kilometers apart, they communicated through a lawyer.

When Eva received her money, she realized two things. She had definitely given up her childhood, her memories, the seemingly carefree part of her life that was supposed to protect her from everything bad. She realized that she had to go back to Bratislava.

She felt remorse from the people they were staying with. She tried to escape again, to eat as little as possible so as not to harm them. She would lock herself in that cold room so as not to bother anyone. Later, her daughter came to see her and they would sit there together for days, because when they went outside so as not to be met, there was always something wrong with it.

Eva promised herself then that no one would ever lock them up anywhere again. First it was her mother, then her husband, the acquaintances they went to, and finally this. She always felt like she was in a madhouse, because the situations they were putting her in would not happen under normal circumstances and with normal people.

Her father protected her from her mother, who temporarily created an asylum for her. Years later, she sold part of this asylum to pay for her ticket to freedom.

*

She didn't tell anyone where she was going. Why? They wouldn't help her anyway, and she wouldn't needlessly inform them about what she would do to survive with her daughter, because she didn't know herself. She always knew only the next step, never the end of the journey.

From one day to the next, she arranged to rent a studio apartment. In the evening, she also listened to opinions about her interpreted by some strangers loud enough for her to hear them in the next room and to warn them against any contact with her. They couldn't hurt Eva anymore, she was used to isolation, trained by a mother who dissuaded her friends, a man who went around and wrote to her friends, former acquaintances, a colleague and her relatives who wouldn't let her go anywhere at all, making excuses about the pandemic, putting on two masks, but at the same time going swimming in the sea, riding go-karts and visiting complete strangers.

The next day, early in the morning, they left. In the city, she bought breakfast and something to take with her. They ate in the car again, this time because of the pandemic measures that did not allow them to eat outside without masks on their faces.

They traveled across the country. The districts were closed, or before they were closed, because they met almost no one on the way across the country. Fortunately, not even the police. The sun was shining on their way and Eva hoped that they would have somewhere to wash and sleep in the evening.

In the house under the mountain, they could wash once or twice a week, because the connection had not been made. They carried water in tanks or had it brought to them from the city. She wanted to be clean. She always liked to return to Bratislava for this reason. In the makeshifts, which, although temporary, last the longest, she hated that she could not change them. It was always about adapting and suffering something that did not suit her, and the only ending to the story was when she finally started living her life on her own.

Although they were in a completely unsuitable studio apartment, it was the best thing that could have happened to them in a while. Eva had no job and couldn't afford to pay rent for a bigger apartment. She thought it would only be temporary, that in a few months something would happen and they would be able to leave. It didn't happen. They didn't leave after a few months.

Eva would have to ask her husband's permission for any move with the child, and he would never do that. That's why they couldn't officially leave anywhere. However, they would have to be tested for any move, and Eva didn't want to expose herself or her daughter to that.

*

One morning, her daughter was swollen and with a lot of toothache, she was jumping around the castle, as they called their asylum in the jungle. She went to get a hundred euros from a friend, for whom she had done something a while ago, and when she had paid a little more, the tooth could have been pulled out.

The pain drove them to the ambulance too early, so they walked around the neighborhood. Eva, immersed in her thoughts, received her daughter's announcement - Look, an English school. Eva didn't pay attention to it, because it was clear that she wasn't up for it.

The children were just getting on the bus and talking in English. She only noticed the sound behind the scenes and kept thinking. A few days later, she found an ad that they were looking for someone at that particular school. She didn't pay any more attention to it, but the ad came again. Okay, she said to herself and wrote back. Everything was arranged very quickly and she could get on, and after some time her daughter also came to see her.

It was strange. She sensed a kind of cycle in their stay in Bratislava. When they arrived there, her daughter had a kindergarten in the exact same part of the city, and now, after long and turbulent years, they were back there again. Until when? - she asked herself.

Eva worked in two schools and in a law firm to pay for everything. She still perceived her marriage vows and some kind of imaginary dysfunctional union as a great burden that she decided to get rid of. She found the forms and submitted an application, which left Bratislava again for her favorite district court, directly into the hands of statistician Etelka. By the time the toothy businesswoman with children had recovered, Eva was already ready and in a fighting mood. She clearly knew that she would leave the district court divorced and would never again waste time on something as undignified as her stay at the district court had been for her.

She arrived first, even though she had driven two hundred kilometers. Toothy arrived later, even though it was just around the corner, but she was all the better prepared. Her preparation for the hearing consisted of arranging a judge who would be on her side. She remembered the judge her husband had been talking about from the beginning, but only now did they manage to successfully arrange it. Toothy would probably not have come to the hearing without her judge.

Eva looked again at the elaborate show of "justice" that had not come to the hearing. Not only was her eyes covered, but she was probably tied up somewhere and tightly bound. Eva didn't care. She sat across from Toothy, listening to her nonsense about how unadaptable she was and waiting for her to at least look at her. She didn't look. Like a turtle with a small head under its shell, she read from the papers in front of her. Eva couldn't laugh, but when the toothy interpreted her husband's nonsense the same nonsense Eva had heard when he first got divorced, which meant it was more than twenty years ago, she knew she had to agree to everything in order to get rid of it all as soon as possible. Eva didn't even resist the judge's ridicule. Yes, she bought herself and her daughter very expensive vitamins, which she was reproached for, so that her soon-to-be ex-husband wouldn't have to pay higher alimony, but she didn't have to sit there now in a mask like a cold judge who shouldn't even be there, but she had to... They could kick as much as they wanted; a person who's already had everything taken away has nothing to lose; Eva wanted to be divorced and she was.

When she returned, she felt as if she was going home from work and not from the divorce court. Her car was parked near the gym where she used to go. She liked it there, but the time when she liked to wander the streets of the small town was already in the past. She didn't call anyone to say she was coming. She didn't call anyone to say she was there.

She went to the district court so often that she felt like she worked there. She tried cases full-time. Unlike the boys who worked at the courthouse, she didn't get paid for it. There had been quite a few of them there in four years, and she knew most of them by sight, most of them remembered Eva.

Only one, a former friend, no longer remembered her. Until she brought her husband to town, they talked, went to sit, to talk. Before one hearing, he talked only to her husband in the hallway, he didn't answer Eve's greetings. When they were finished, he walked past her and disappeared from her life as he had appeared in it.

No one knew she was in town, no one knew she was at court. As she had come, so she had left. Quietly. She bought yogurt at the grocery store and hurried back because even her daughter didn't know what she had done that day. She found out about it in the middle of a conversation, but it wasn't information that would affect anything in her life. It kept spinning, whether they had or not, Eva simply had to arrange it so that it would be.

*

With the divorce, something seemed to loosen up in her personal life as well. She fell in love. She finally felt love. Although it was unfulfilled, it was beautiful. He left and he was missed very much.

For the second time, with a new job, a chance for love came into her life again, the same wonderful feeling when everything is possible and life is simple and wonderful, but there was an obstacle that Eva could not overcome and did not want to. He was married. She left in anticipation of a third chance at life, the true, only and great love that would embrace the whole world. He would embrace Eva, the first, the last and the only one. She would be the first, the last and the only one.